THE BOLD, BAD BOYS!

and other stories

Illustrated by
Paul Crompton

World International Publishing Limited
Manchester

Published in Great Britain by World International
Publishing Limited,
An Egmont Company, Egmont House, PO Box 111,
Great Ducie Street,
Manchester M60 3BL.
Printed in Italy.

British Library Cataloguing in Publication Data
Blyton, Enid 1897–1968
The bold, bad boys! and other stories.
1. Title II. Series
823.912[J]

ISBN 0–7498–0317–7

Cover illustration by Robin Lawrie

Contents

Enid Blyton

Enid Blyton was born in London in 1897. Her childhood was spent in Beckenham, Kent, and as a child she began to write poems, stories and plays. She trained to be a teacher but she devoted her whole life to being a children's author. Her first book was a collection of poems for children, published in 1922. In 1926 she began to write a weekly magazine for children called *Sunny Stories*, and it was here that many of her most popular stories and characters first appeared. The magazine was immensely popular and in 1953 it became *The Enid Blyton Magazine*.

She wrote more than 600 books for children and many of her most popular series are still published all over the world. Her books have been translated into over 30 languages. Enid Blyton died in 1968.

The bold, bad boys!

Derek and Tom loved to go down and play beside the river. They liked watching the boats go by, and when a steamer sailed along in midstream, making quite big waves break against the banks, they shouted with joy.

"Daddy, can't we have a boat of our own?" begged Derek. "Lots of the boys we know have. Why can't we?"

"For a very good reason," said Daddy. "You can't swim yet! I tried to teach you last summer, but you both cried because the water was cold, and Tom yelled when I held him up and tried to make him do the arm-strokes."

The two boys looked rather ashamed. "If you'd let us have a boat, we promise we will learn to swim this summer," said Derek.

"Oh, no!" said Daddy. "I'll promise you a boat when you have learnt to swim. That's the right way to put it."

The boys went off, rather sulky. "Lots of people who can't swim have boats," said Tom. "How can we have adventures, and go rowing off to find them, if we haven't got a boat. Daddy's mean."

"Never mind," said Derek. "We'll have a good time paddling. We'll call ourselves The Bold, Bad Boys and we'll look for adventures every single day. We'll be pirates and smugglers, and we'll be very bold and daring."

So they were. They became a great nuisance to the moorhens by the river, and the big swans hissed at them as they sailed grandly by. But when the cows came down to stand in the shallow part of the river, The Bold, Bad Boys ran away. They were rather afraid of cows!

Now, one day, when the two boys were sitting by the water, splashing it with their feet, they saw something coming down the river. It wasn't a boat. It wasn't a bird. What could it be?

"It's a barrel! An empty barrel, floating along by itself!" cried Derek. "If only we could get it, Tom. We could play smugglers properly if we had a barrel of our own! We could even hide in it."

They watched the barrel. It came bobbing along – and floated to where a low branch stretched out from the bank over the water. There it caught and stopped.

"Look, look!" cried Derek. "That branch has caught it. Oh, Tom, let's be really bold and crawl out on that branch and get the barrel. I think the water is shallow there, and maybe we could get on the barrel and push it over to the bank."

So, feeling very bold and daring, the two boys crawled along the branch to the barrel. Derek leaned down and caught hold of it.

"Tom, can you get on to the barrel whilst I hold it?" he said. "Quick, in case I have to let go. That's right. Oh, good, you're riding the barrel! Will it take me too, do you think?"

Tom had dropped neatly on to the barrel, and was now riding it astride, grinning happily. Derek dropped down beside him.

Now they were both on the barrel. "Work hard with your feet and we'll get it to the bank," said Derek. But, alas, as soon as they left the tree branch, the barrel, instead of going towards the bank, got caught by the midstream current and swung out into deep water. Then it began floating merrily down the river with the two boys riding it!

Tom screamed. "Derek, Derek! We're out in deep water. We'll drown!"

"Not if we cling to the barrel," said Derek, going rather white. "Hold on, Tom. Don't let go whatever you do. Oh,

gracious, we're going fast!"

"I feel sick, I feel sick," wailed Tom. "I want to be rescued. Oooooooooh!"

Derek was scared, too. He clung to the bobbing barrel and looked round to see if any boat was about. Not one was anywhere to be seen. So on they bobbed and on and on.

Tom was crying.

Then suddenly a fisherman by the river saw them. "Help, help!" cried Derek. "Save us!"

In the greatest astonishment the fisherman ran to a small boat nearby and got into it. With three or four strong pulls at the oars he was soon alongside the barrel. He pulled the boys into the boat. Tom burst into wails.

"We were nearly drowned. Take me home to Mummy."

The fisherman rowed to shore. He found out where the boys lived and took them both back, wet and scared. Daddy came out when he saw them.

"Whatever's the matter?" he said.

"Have you fallen in the river?"

"No, oh no!" wailed Tom. "We saw a barrel floating down and we crawled out on a tree branch to it . . ."

"And got on it, meaning to take it to the bank, and it floated away with us," said Derek.

"I rescued them in time," said the fisherman, winking at Daddy. "Seems to me they're strange boys, not liking an adventure. Most boys are looking out for one every day."

"So do Tom and Derek," said their father. "In fact, I believe they call themselves The Bold, Bad Boys, and half the time they're smugglers and pirates. And when a little adventure like this comes along, they yell and howl and can't bear it! Well, well, well!"

"Why didn't they swim to shore?" asked the fisherman, surprised to hear all this.

"I'm sorry to have to tell you – but both boys are too scared to learn to swim," said Daddy, solemnly. "They want a boat – and yet they can't swim!"

"Well, they had a barrel for a boat, and they didn't seem to like that at all," said the fisherman. "I reckon a boat would be wasted on them, sir."

"Just what I think," said Daddy. "Well, thanks for rescuing them. Maybe one day they will welcome an adventure when they get one, instead of howling about it."

"Thanks for rescuing us, sir," said Derek, his face very red indeed. He felt so ashamed. To think they were the two Bold, Bad Boys, always looking out for an adventure, and now they had behaved like this!

Derek took Tom into the garden into their secret corner. "We're going to learn to swim!" he told Tom fiercely. "Do you hear, Tom? And there's to be no moaning and groaning about it. We're going to make Daddy proud of us for a change!"

Well, the last time I saw Derek and Tom they were in a small, neat boat of their own, rowing out on the river. So I knew they had learnt to swim, and could really look for exciting adventures. Do you know what they have called their boat? Guess! It's called *The Bold, Bad Boys*!

They didn't want him

Somebody had come to live in the house next door to Alec and Winnie. They wondered if there were any children, so they watched to see.

"Oh! Only one little boy," said Alec, who was ten. "He's too small to play with."

"Tiny children are a nuisance," said Winnie, who was eight, quite forgetting that she had once been tiny herself.

Their mother made friends with the new people next door. Their name was White, and the little boy was Harry White. He was six.

"Do you think your two children would mind letting Harry go to the park to play with them until he makes friends

of his own age?" asked Mrs White.

"Of course he can go with them," said Mrs Lane, the other children's mother. "They will be pleased."

But, dear me, they weren't a bit pleased! They were really horrid to Harry when they took him to the park next day. They laughed at him because he couldn't run as fast as they did. They laughed at him when he couldn't catch a ball. He wasn't at all happy.

The day after that, Mrs White again asked if Winnie and Alec would take Harry with them, as she was going to be very busy putting up her new curtains, and she wanted Harry out of the way. So off went the three children, Winnie and Alec looking sulky.

"You're a nuisance," said Alec to poor Harry. "If you think we're going to walk as slowly as you, you're wrong. And we aren't going to waste all our morning playing with you either – we're going to play with our own friends, who aren't babies like you!"

Harry tried to hurry after them to keep up with them — and down he fell flat on his face! He cut his knees, and felt very unhappy. He didn't cry, because he didn't want the others to think he was a baby again. He sat down and mopped his knees with his hanky.

"Come on!" said Alec to Winnie. "Don't wait for him! We'll slip away whilst he's sitting down. We can easily go round the park and find him when it's time to go home."

So they ran right away to the other end of the park and left Harry all alone. When he looked up, they were gone.

Harry didn't know what to do. He did not dare to go home alone, because there were too many roads to cross. Supposing he had to stay in the park all day and all night? That would be dreadful!

He felt so lonely and his knees hurt him so much that he couldn't help two tears squeezing out of his eyes. They rolled down his cheeks.

A little girl playing nearby suddenly saw him sitting on the grass. She spoke to her brother.

"Look, George! Isn't that the little boy we said 'hello' to the other day – the one who has just moved in across the road from us? He's all alone. Do you suppose he is lost? He isn't much older than our little Mollie at home! Our mother wouldn't let *her* come out all alone!"

"We'll go and see what's the matter," said George, who was a big boy of ten. So he and his sister Sue went up to Harry. "What's the matter, little boy?" asked Sue.

"I've fallen down and hurt my knees, and I haven't got a big enough hanky to tie them up," said Harry. "And the two children who were with me don't like me because I'm little, so they've run away and left me. I don't know where they are, and I daren't go home alone, because there are too many roads to cross."

"What mean children!" said George.

"Well, look here, those knees of yours want bathing. Shall we take you home and get them bathed and bandaged? Then you can come back to the park with us if you like – or come home with us and play with our little sister Mollie. You might have seen her. She's about the same size as you. We live just across the road from your new house. Do you remember, we shouted 'hello' to you the other day?"

"Oh, I remember," said Harry, getting up. "I would like you to take me home, thank you." He took Sue's hand. Together the three of them walked safely home. Mrs White was surprised to see Harry with the two children, but they soon explained to her what had happened.

"If you could bathe his knees for him, we would look after him for you," said George. "We often have to look after our little sister Mollie, so you could trust us. We have a big garden at home, and I expect our mother would let Harry come and play with Mollie there. We live just across the road. Look – there's our mother in the front garden!"

"Oh – I know her," said Mrs White. "She came and spoke to me yesterday and asked me if she could help me at all. She knows how busy people are when they move house. Her children are as kind as she is! Thank you, my dears. Would you all like to come to tea this afternoon with Harry? I shall have finished putting up my curtains then, and we could have a lovely tea together."

"We'll go and ask our mother," said Sue. So off they ran – and of course their mother said yes.

Harry didn't go out to play any more that morning, because his knees hurt him. He wondered what Alec and Winnie would say when they couldn't find him in the park.

They were very frightened when half-past twelve came, and they couldn't find Harry. They hunted round and round

the park for him, getting hot and tired
– but not a sign of Harry was to be seen!

"Whatever shall we do?" said Alec
in dismay. "I daren't go home without
him."

"Perhaps he went home by himself
and got knocked down," said Winnie,
looking frightened. "Oh, Alec – what
shall we do?"

Well, there was nothing to be done
but to go home – and home they went.
They ran into the kitchen where their
mother was waiting to get their dinner.
They were very late, and she was cross.

"And what do you mean by leaving
Harry all by himself in the park?"
she scolded. "I've heard all about it
from Mrs White. Two strange children
brought the poor little fellow home, with
his knees badly cut. I feel ashamed of
you."

Alec and Winnie ate their dinner
without a word. And didn't they stare
that afternoon when they saw Sue,
Mollie and George going to tea with

Harry! They knew them, because they all went to school together.

"I say," said Alec to George next day, "don't you think that Harry is a cry-baby?"

"No, I don't," said George. "He's a nice little boy. We went to tea there yesterday and we had chocolate biscuits, orange jelly, and ginger-cake. And afterwards we played with Harry's train. Do you know he's got a railway line that goes all round his bedroom, and two of the finest trains I've ever seen! My word, we did have fun!"

Alec stared at George in dismay. He loved trains. He felt jealous of George. After all, he had known Harry first.

"It's no use you looking like that!" said Sue with a laugh. "You were mean to Harry – and you can be sure he doesn't want to share his lovely toys with you! You didn't want him – and you can't blame him if he doesn't want *you*!"

Harry *didn't* want them. He made friends with Sue and George and Mollie, and shared all his lovely toys with them. Alec saw George driving Harry's big tricycle down the street. He saw Sue riding Harry's car – and he saw Mollie going to tea each week to play with Harry's railway.

"I'm not a bit sorry for you," said their mother, when they grumbled to her that Harry never asked them to tea or to play. "You had a fine chance to make friends with Harry, and you didn't. Perhaps you'll be nicer another time!"

Perhaps they will!

The big red engine

Morris had a big red engine. It was made of strong wood, and was big enough to carry somebody if they sat on the boiler.

Morris liked to go to the top of the hill with his big red engine, sit on the boiler, and then let the engine carry him downhill at top speed. It really was fun.

But he wouldn't let anyone else do that. He didn't like sharing his toys. Some children don't – and, of course, nobody likes them much then.

Sometimes he went shopping for his mummy, and then he put all the goods into his engine cab, taking them home like that, pulling on a piece of rope he had tied to the funnel. That was fun.

"Please do let me put my shopping into your engine cab," Molly said to him one day. "There's plenty of room. These potatoes are so heavy."

"No. My engine only carries *my* goods," said Morris.

"You're mean and selfish," said Molly. "Nobody likes you! One day you'll find your engine gone, and it will serve you right!"

"What do you mean?" said Morris, in alarm. But Molly had gone, carrying her heavy bag of potatoes.

Now, the next week Morris did such a lot of shopping for his mummy that she gave him some money to spend. He thought he would go and buy some sweets. Yes, he would buy some big humbugs – the black stripy ones that lasted a very long time.

He met James and Betty and Lennie. He showed them his money. "I'm going to buy a bag of humbugs," he said.

"Will you give me one?" asked little Betty.

"No. Why should I?" said Morris. "You've never given *me* a sweet, have you? Get out of my way, please. I'm going downhill to the sweet shop on my red engine. You watch me chuff down at top speed!"

The three children watched Morris get astride the boiler of the engine, put up his feet and then, hey presto, the engine rolled away merrily down the hill to the sweet shop. Morris shouted "Chuff-chuff-chuff" as he went. He felt rather proud.

He came to the sweet shop. There was a pram outside and a bicycle, too. There wasn't any room to park his engine. So he left it outside the shop next door. Then in he went to choose his sweets.

The shop had no humbugs that day. Morris looked round at all the bottles and boxes. What should he have then? It really was difficult to choose. He thought about it for a long time and the shop assistant got impatient.

At last he chose some toffees, and the

assistant weighed them out. Then she looked out of the window.

"My word! Look at the rain!" she said. "You had better wait till it stops, or you will get soaked."

So Morris stayed in the shop and waited till the rain stopped. It was a nice shop to wait in. He looked at every kind of sweet there was.

"The rain's stopped now," he said at last, and out he went to get his engine.

But it wasn't there! There was nothing there. The pram had gone, so had the bicycle. And so, most certainly, had his red engine.

"It's those horrid children!" he said. "Lennie, Betty and James. *They've* taken it! Just because I wouldn't share my sweets with them. I expect Molly told them to take it. She said I'd find it gone one day."

He saw Lennie, Betty and James coming out of a shop farther up the road – and yes, Molly was with them.

They had taken it, they had hidden it! He raced after them, shouting.

"Where's my engine? What have you done with it? Where is it?"

The four children turned round at once, looking surprised. "*We* haven't got your engine," said Molly. "Don't shout at us like that."

"You have! I left it outside those shops down there, and when I came out it was gone. You've taken it, you know you have – just because I wouldn't share my sweets!"

"Don't be silly," said Molly. "We wouldn't do such a horrid thing as take your engine. Not that you don't deserve it! You do! Now go away – you're making Betty cry."

Well, Morris stamped and raged, but it wasn't a bit of good. Nobody told him anything about his red engine. "I'm going home," he shouted. "I shall tell my daddy. I shall get you all punished! I'm very upset."

He stamped off home, crying now,

because he loved his red engine and it was terrible to lose it so suddenly. The other children went the other way. Betty was crying, too, because Morris had scared her. Molly comforted her.

"He's just a horrid, selfish boy. You don't need to worry, Betty. It serves him right to lose his engine."

Now, just as they passed the sweet shop, a woman came out of the shop next door – and what a surprising thing, she carried Morris's red engine! She set it down and then called to the four children.

"Does this belong to you, children? I found it outside my shop in the pouring rain, and it's such a lovely toy that I took it inside the shop out of the wet. But now I can't find out who it belongs to!"

"Oh! It's Morris's engine!" cried Molly. "He thought *we'd* taken it. He's awfully cross about it. I'd better take it home to him."

"No, don't," said James. "It will do

him good to think it's lost. Let him be miserable."

"Well, he deserves to be, but I think even if *he's* horrid *we* needn't be," said Molly. "I know how glad I am when I get back something I've lost. Come on, let's take it to Morris."

So they all took it to Morris's house, taking it in turn to pull it along by the rope. Nobody quite liked to ride on the boiler. They came to Morris's house and went round to the garden door.

Mr Felton, Morris's daddy, opened the door and exclaimed in surprise at the engine.

"Please," said Molly, "we've brought back the engine. The shop lady next door to the sweet shop took it into her place when it poured with rain, and then she couldn't find out who it belonged to. Morris left it outside her shop, you see. She told us all about it."

"I see," said Mr Felton. He called Morris. "Morris, come here. Your engine is back."

Morris came running. He pulled his engine indoors at once and glared fiercely at the four children.

"So you've brought it back, you horrid things! Where did you hide it? How dare you take my engine?"

"Morris," said his father, in a cold sort of voice, "somebody kindly took it into their shop out of the rain, and these four children found out by accident, and have brought it back for you. These are the children you have been saying horrid things about, and have refused to share your sweets with – or so you told me. You said they had stolen your engine and didn't deserve a single sweet. What have you to say?"

Morris went scarlet. His mouth opened – he hadn't a word to say.

"I think I'll give your engine to these four children," said Mr Felton. "And your sweets, too. I am surprised you can't even say you are sorry, or thank them for bringing it back. I'm ashamed of you."

He took the engine from Morris and pushed it towards Molly. But she shook her head.

"No, thank you," she said. "We don't want it. We don't want the sweets either. We only brought back the engine because we know how horrid it is to lose something you like. Goodbye, Morris."

The four of them went down the path. "I wouldn't like a boy like Morris if *I* was a daddy!" said James.

"I wonder what his daddy will say to him now," said Lennie. "I wonder if he'll let Morris keep his engine."

I don't know what Mr Felton *did* say to Morris – but I do know that he gives all the other children rides on his engine now, and takes Molly's shopping home in the cab, and shares every single bag of sweets all round. In fact, you wouldn't know that he was the same boy. So perhaps it was a very good thing that the shop lady took his red engine in out of the rain and made Morris think that he had lost it!

The boy who scribbled

Bobby was a great nuisance wherever he went, because he scribbled over everything! He always took his pencils and chalks with him – and, dear me, how he scribbled on walls, seats, and pavements!

"Bobby, it is very bad manners to scribble over things like that," said his mother.

"Bobby, you've spoilt our nice new garden seat by scribbling your name all over it," said his aunt, crossly.

"Bobby, if you scribble on your desk again, you will stay in after school and write out 'I must not scribble', one hundred times," said his teacher.

But Bobby went on scribbling. You

may have seen some of his scribbles, for he scribbled everywhere. Sometimes he wrote horrid things. Once, when Ellen wouldn't lend him her book, he wrote "Ellen is a selfish girl" all over her wall in white chalk. Her mother was very angry.

The policeman was angry too, because Bobby's town tried to keep the streets clean and tidy, there were litter-bins everywhere and nobody was supposed to make a mess on the walls or fences. But Bobby simply couldn't help it.

His mother took away his chalks and his pencils. But Bobby found a sharp white stone and wrote all over the pavement with it. He was cross with George, so he wrote "George is a horrid boy" three times. George was so angry when he saw it.

Now, one day Bobby went for a picnic in a wood all by himself. He had a basket packed with goodies, and he meant to have a good time. He found a little path he hadn't seen before, and off he went into the very heart of the wood. And when he came there he found a pretty little whitewashed house, with a neat whitewashed wall around it, and bright flowers growing in the garden!

Bobby was most astonished. He stared at the house in surprise. "I didn't know anyone lived in this wood," he said to himself. "What a dear little house! I think I'll have my picnic here, and then I can go and ask for a drink of water at the house if I'm thirsty."

So he sat down nearby and undid his basket of food. There were sandwiches, cake, and apples, with a bar of chocolate to finish the meal. Bobby enjoyed it very much.

"Now for a drink!" he said. He got up and went to the little white gate. He opened it, went up the neat path, and knocked at the little white door.

But nobody came. Nobody seemed to be in the house at all. "Bother!" said Bobby. "Just when I wanted a drink!"

He went round the back to see if anyone was there. The dustbin was there, and the coal-house. A piece of coal lay on the ground. Bobby picked it up.

And then you can guess what that naughty little boy did! He began to scribble over the white walls of the cottage with the coal. He drew some little men. He drew a house with chimneys. He wrote his own name again and again – Robert William Tomkins, Robert William Tomkins.

The coal made very black lines which showed up well on the house. When Bobby had finished scribbling on the white walls, he began to scribble on the walls of the garden. He wrote "This is a silly house. There is no one to give me a drink." What a thing to do!

Then he wrote two or three things about his school friends. He put "Harry has carroty hair. Jane has rabbit-teeth. John is a cry-baby."

Just as he was finishing this, he

heard a noise. He looked up and saw six little pixie men come through the wood. They hadn't seen him, because he was sitting beside the garden wall.

Bobby felt frightened. *Six* little men! They might be very angry with him for scribbling. He looked at the house – yes, he had done a dreadful lot of scribbles there. The naughty little boy quietly picked up his basket and, bending down to hide himself behind the wall, ran off into the wood without being seen.

When the six little men came up to their house they stared in the greatest horror at their white walls, which were now all spoilt with the black coal-marks.

"Who has done this shocking thing?" said the chief little man in anger.

"Just look!" cried another. "All the way round our lovely house! Some horrid nuisance of a scribbler has been here."

"If only we knew who it was!" said the chief man. "I would punish him well!"

"I can tell you who he is," said the third little man, and he pointed to where Bobby had written his name again and again – Robert William Tomkins, Robert William Tomkins. "Look, that's his name!"

"Ha!" said the chief man, looking stern. "So that's who he is. I've heard of him before. Well, he'll be sorry for this!"

"Yes," said the little men, going to get cloths and water to wash their walls. "Yes – he'll be sorry for this!"

The little men soon found out where Bobby lived. And then one of them kept near Bobby all day long, although the boy didn't know it. The little men watched all he did. They saw him smack Nora. They saw him throw a stone at a cat. They heard him being rude to old Mrs Lucy. Oh, they soon found out quite a lot about Bobby!

And then strange things began to happen. One day when Bobby and his mother came home from a walk, they found their green front door painted

42

all over with big red letters. And this is what was written on the door – "BOBBY IS A HORRID RUDE BOY."

"Good gracious!" said his mother. "Look at that! Whoever has written that on our front door? We must get it off at once."

But they couldn't get it off, because it was painted with magic paint! So there it was for everyone to read when they went by. Bobby was angry and ashamed. He remembered that he had been rude to old Mrs Lucy, and he was careful to be polite the next time in case she had written the message!

The next thing that happened was a long message, painted in bright green on the pavement outside Bobby's house:

"BOBBY IS VERY UNKIND AND SELFISH. HE HAS BIG EARS. HE IS UNKIND TO ANIMALS! HA, HA!"

"Oh dear!" said Bobby's mother, nearly in tears. "Who *can* have done that on our pavement? Bobby, how I wish you had never had that dreadful habit of scribbling over everything! Now you see what has happened! Other people are scribbling things about you too."

Bobby was red with shame. How dreadful that everyone who came by should read those things about him! He went to look at his ears. Yes – they *were* big. Well, he had teased Harry about his red hair, so perhaps it was Harry who had painted the horrid message on the pavement, and had put that Bobby had big ears.

Harry said he hadn't done anything of the sort. "I'm not a silly scribbler like you!" he cried. "All I can say is that it serves you right for being such a horrid scribbler yourself!"

The next day the nice red walls of the house were painted white with comical pictures of Bobby and his big ears. Bobby cried and cried, he was so ashamed. His mother and father went to the policeman about the scribbles, and begged for his help.

"Well, I don't feel much inclined to help that boy of yours," said the policeman. "I've had plenty of trouble from *him* over scribbling on walls and pavements, I can tell you. If you ask me, I think this just serves him right!"

But all the same the policeman kept an eye on Bobby's house that night – and when he saw six funny little men creeping up with pails and brushes, he walked up to them with a large frown.

"Now then, what's all this?" he began in a very deep voice – but to his great surprise every single one of the little men vanished! Yes, disappeared into thin air, and not even a paintbrush was left!

That was the end of the scribbling on Bobby's house. The little men came no more. Bobby's daddy had his house repainted, and the front door, too, and sent someone to clean the pavement outside. Then he spoke sternly to Bobby.

"All this has happened because of

your horrid scribbling habits," said Mr Tomkins. "Have you anything to say to me about them, Bobby?"

"I'll never scribble anywhere again, Daddy," said Bobby in a low voice. And since then he never has. I'd hate to have horrid things scribbled about me by those six little men, wouldn't you?

The boy who wanted a pet

There was once a boy called Harry. He had no brothers or sisters, so he was often lonely.

"If I had a dog – or a cat – or even a rabbit in a hutch, it would be something to play with and love," thought Harry. "I'll ask Mummy again. If I ask her often enough, perhaps she'll say yes."

So he went to find his mother. "Mummy," he said, "I know you always say no – but please this time do say yes! Can I have a puppy?"

"Certainly not," said his mother. "It would grow into a noisy, barking dog – and bring mud into the house all the time."

"Well, can I have a kitten then?" said

Harry. "Do, do say yes to a kitten! It wouldn't bark or bring mud into the house."

"Perhaps not. But it would grow into a cat, and all cats are thieves," said his mother. "It would steal food from the larder and jump up on the table. I know cats!"

"Well, a rabbit, then, Mummy – a dear little soft, fluffy rabbit with a woffly nose?" said Harry. "I would keep it in a cage and look after it myself."

"You wouldn't look after it," said his mother. "You'd get tired of it, and then *I* should have to see to it, and I'm much too busy. I might even have to make it into a pie."

Mummy was joking, but Harry thought she meant it. He went off without another word. He couldn't, couldn't keep any pet that might be eaten! Well, he would have to do without, that was all.

His mother saw that he was upset, and she called after him. "Harry! Get out your new little garage and arrange your cars in it. You'll like that. Take it down the garden – it's warm enough in the shed for you to play with it there."

Harry cheered up. He went into his playroom and fetched his two garages. One was small and old, and needed painting. The other was big and brand-new, and would hold all his tiny little cars. It would be fun to change them over from the old garage to the new one.

He carried both garages down to the shed in the garden, and the little cars, too. The winter sun came into the shed and it was nice and warm. Harry began to sort out his cars.

He talked to himself, as he always did. "This car can go into that corner of the new garage. And the two buses can go over here together. And the little lorry can stand next to the butcher's van. And, let me see – where shall I put the fire-engine? That ought to be near one of the entrances, in case it is called out suddenly."

He played happily with his cars till dinner-time. Then he carefully carried his new garage indoors with all the cars and vans neatly arranged inside. Mother thought it looked really lovely.

"Don't go and fetch your old garage just now," she said. "Dinner is on the table. Go down afterwards, lock the shed, and bring the garage back then."

So after dinner Harry went down the garden again. He carried his old garage out of the shed and set it down on the grass while he locked up the shed. He was just going to pick up his garage when he saw a robin standing on the handle of an old garden fork nearby. It sang a bright little song to him, and then flew even nearer, perching on a twig. Harry could almost have touched him!

"Are you hungry?" said Harry. "Is that what you are saying? That you want a few crumbs? Well, follow me up to my house, Robin, and I'll give you some. Come along!"

Harry went slowly to the house, followed by the robin. He forgot all about his old garage, left in the grass. The robin followed him closely, flying from bush to bush after him. Harry was delighted.

He fetched some crumbs and came out-of-doors again. The robin was still there. Harry scattered some crumbs round his feet, and the robin flew down at once. Once it even perched on Harry's foot, and he hardly dared to breathe in case he frightened it off!

It wasn't until he was going to bed that night that he remembered he had left his old garage down the garden in the grass. "Bother!" he said. "I'd better fetch it. If Daddy finds it there tomorrow morning he'll be cross with me."

So Harry put on his coat and slipped out into the garden. It was quite dark now. He had to go slowly because he was afraid he would walk into the bushes. Ah – that big black shape must be the shed. Now – where was his garage? Why, oh why hadn't he brought his torch!

He suddenly stopped. He had heard a peculiar sound – like a car hooting. But it must be a very tiny car because it was a very tiny hoot. It came from the ground nearby. Harry looked carefully all round.

He saw the lights of what must be a very small car indeed – and then another pair of lights. They were moving along, too. The cars, whoever they belonged to, were being driven carefully over the grass.

Harry went cautiously over and knelt down. He was most amazed by what he saw! His old garage was there in the grass, where he had left it. But the doors were open, there was a light inside – and two tiny cars were backing in, side by side!

"I say!" said Harry, loudly and excitedly. "I SAY! Who are you? And what are you doing in my garage?"

The cars stopped very suddenly indeed. A tiny head leaned sideways out of one of the drivers' seats. Harry could see it quite clearly.

"Hallo!" said the head. "Are you Harry?"

"Yes," said Harry, astonished. "But how did you know?"

"The robin told us," said the head, nodding. "He said you were kind, and gave him some crumbs when he was hungry. He said you wouldn't mind us having your old garage for our cars."

Harry bent down even closer. He was so excited and astonished that he could hardly breathe. He saw that the little head belonged to a small man with a beard. Another man very like him was in the other car. He poked his head out too.

"But who *are* you?" said Harry. "And why do you want my old garage?"

"I'm Bip Brownie, and he's Bop," said Bip. "We do a big business running round the rabbit-holes in our cars, taking odds and ends of carrots and things. But we haven't got a garage, and in this cold weather we're afraid our cars will freeze up. Then we suddenly found this garage in the grass . . ."

"And the robin told us it was your old one, and you were kind and wouldn't mind us having it," said Bop, suddenly joining in. "But of course we'll not use it now. I expect you've come to fetch it, haven't you?"

"Well, yes, I have," said Harry. "But I've got a beautiful new one now, so I don't need this one. You can have it for your cars. I'd *love* you to! I'd love to think my old garage was having *real* little cars being driven in and out."

"Thank you very much indeed," said Bip, and he backed his car right in. Harry bent right down to look inside the garage, and saw that the two brownies had lighted a tiny candle there. It really looked very exciting inside his garage, with two cars parked there, their headlights still on.

"Listen," said Harry, suddenly. "I think I'd better come back early in the morning and carry the garage to a safer place. My daddy might find it here. It's no good telling him or anyone that two brownies are using it – they just wouldn't believe me. I'll come and put it in a very safe place where no one will find it. Then you can use it as much as you like."

"Oh, *thank* you!" said Bip, switching off his car lights. "That would be grand. There's a little nut-copse not far off where hazel trees grow thickly. That would be a fine place for our garage – it's nice and near all the rabbit-holes, too."

"Isn't he a *kind* boy!" said Bop, coming out of the garage and shutting the doors. "The robin was quite right about him. Bip, we ought to do something in return, you know."

"Yes, we ought," said Bip. "Anything you specially want, Harry? A magic pencil? Or a story in a book that never ends? Or an ice-cream that never finishes? Or . . ."

Harry laughed. "Oh dear – don't tell me any more! There's only *one* thing I really want, and I'll never have it."

"What's that?" asked Bip and Bop together.

"Well, I want a *pet*," said Harry. "But it would have to be a pet that wasn't noisy, or dirty, or a thief, or wanted a lot of looking after, or could be eaten."

"Impossible!" said the brownies, together. "Think of something else and tell us tomorrow morning!"

"All right," said Harry. "Well, good-night – I really must go. Your cars will be quite safe now!"

Next morning before breakfast Harry was down the garden again. Where was his garage? Ah, there it was, in the grass. The doors were shut. He knelt down and looked in at the window. Yes – the two tiny cars were still there. Where were Bip and Bop? Perhaps he had better whistle. He didn't need to. The robin had seen him and had already flown to tell Bip and Bop that Harry was there. They appeared the very next minute, running at top speed out of a nearby rabbit-hole.

"Hallo!" they said. "Good boy! You've remembered to come!"

"Of course," said Harry, and carefully lifted up the garage. But the brownies made him put it down again. "No, no," they said. "We'll get our cars out first, and drive in front of you to the nut-copse so that you will know the way."

So they got out their cars and drove in front of Harry, bumping over the grass, hooting at a little mouse who came to see what was happening. Harry followed them, carrying the garage. Soon they came to the little thicket of hazel trees, and Harry carefully put the garage down where they told him. It was well hidden under a bush.

"Thank you," said Bip. "And now, listen! We've found you a pet!"

"One that isn't noisy, or dirty, will never be a thief, doesn't need taking care of, and can't be eaten!" said Bop.

"What is it?" said Harry, astonished.

"Look – there he is!" said Bip – and will you believe it, down from the hazel tree bounded a little red squirrel! He leapt on to Harry's shoulder, and chattered in his ear.

"He's been asleep half the winter," said Bip. "But there's a warm spell on now, so he's woken up to find the nuts he hid. But he can't find them. He's got such a bad memory, you know. So if you like to buy him some nuts, he'll be glad to be your pet – your friend, really."

"*Will* he?" cried Harry, in delight. He stroked the thick fur of the pretty little squirrel, and felt his big, bushy tail. What a lovely, lovely pet!

"He'll frisk in and out of your window, and come when you call him," said Bop. "He'll just want a few nuts, that's all. He'll go on being wild, but he'll be your friend, and he'll come when you call him. His name is Frisky Whiskers."

The squirrel pulled at Harry's ear with tiny little paws. It felt lovely!

"He's the nicest pet in the world!" said Harry, joyfully. "Mother can't possibly mind *him*! Oh, thank you – he's a wonderful exchange for my old garage!"

Well, he was, wasn't he? Harry went off with Frisky on his shoulder, and bought him some fine nuts. Then he took him home for Mother to see. And she loved him too. "The pretty, frisky, dainty little thing!" she said. "But don't think he'll be your pet, Harry. He won't. He's a wild thing, really. I can't imagine why he's suddenly made friends with you."

But he *is* Harry's pet – and his friend and companion, too. He even goes to school with him sometimes, but he's so very, very good that Miss Brown, the teacher, lets him stay in the classroom. Harry's very lucky, isn't he?

The old garage is still in the hazel copse, but the brownies have repainted it, so it looks fine. I know you won't take it if you see it – but do just kneel down and see if Bip's car and Bop's are parked inside!

Peter's Noah's Ark

Peter had a lovely playhouse at the bottom of the garden. He kept all his toys there, his soldiers, his fortress, his teddy bear, his books and his beautiful Noah's Ark with all its animals and birds.

Just outside the playhouse was a little stream, and Peter often used to sail his big boat, his two little boats and his steamer there. He had great fun.

One day his cousin John came to ask if he would go to spend the night with him, and bring all his boats and his steamer.

"I've got a fine pond in my garden," said John. "We'll sail our boats and have a splendid time."

So Peter went to his playhouse and took all his boats. Then he shut the door and off he went with John. The toys felt rather sad, for they knew that no one would play with them that day.

"I do hate it when Peter goes off and leaves us," said the bear. "There's nothing much to do. Toys never have adventures like boys and girls. We just stay here and do nothing unless Peter plays with us. Oh, I *would* like an adventure, wouldn't you?"

"Rather!" cried all the soldiers.

Mr and Mrs Noah looked out of the Ark.

"Perhaps one day we shall all have a fine adventure," they said.

"Pooh!" said everyone, rudely. "*You're* not likely to have adventures with your silly old Ark!"

Mr and Mrs Noah said no more. They knew they were old-fashioned, and they often felt hurt when the other toys laughed at their wooden Ark.

But that night an adventure really

did come to the toys! For just about midnight they heard a great shouting outside, and woke up in a fright. Then someone came knocking at the playhouse door.

"Open, open, in the name of the King of Fairyland!" cried a voice.

The teddy bear ran across the floor and opened the door. Outside stood an elf, wet through and dripping.

"Oh!" he said. "Such a dreadful thing has happened. The King and Queen of Fairyland were going along in their ship down the stream, on a visit to the Prince of Buttercup Land, when suddenly a wind came and blew the ship right over!"

"Good gracious!" cried all the toys in horror. "Are they drowned?"

"No, nobody's drowned," said the elf. "But we're all wet through, and the ship has sunk. We want to know if we can come in here and dry ourselves."

"Of course," said the toys. "Of course! Oh dear, we are dreadfully sorry! We will light the fire in the old dolls' house and you can dry yourselves there."

The soldiers ran to the dolls' house and opened the front door. They quickly lit the fire in the drawing room, and then one of them started the kitchen fire too, and put a jug of cocoa on the stove to warm.

Soon in came the King and Queen, wet through and shivering. They were delighted to see the bright fire, and very soon they were sitting by it, drying themselves. Their little elfin servants dried themselves by the kitchen fire, and poured out tiny cups of hot cocoa, which they took to the King and Queen.

"We are very sorry to hear of your sad plight, Your Majesty," said the teddy bear. "We wish that you could spend the night in the dolls' house, but unfortunately there are no beds. Peter gave them all to a little friend of his one day when she came to play with him."

"Dear, dear, what a pity!" said the Queen. "But anyway, I'm afraid we mustn't stop after we have dried ourselves. We must get on with our journey, or the Prince of Buttercup Land will be very much worried about us."

"Perhaps there is a boat here we might borrow?" asked the King.

"Oh, Your Majesty, Peter has taken both his big boat and his little boat to his cousin's," cried the toys in dismay.

"Well, is there a toy steamer we might have?" asked the King.

"Peter's taken that too!" said the teddy bear. "Oh, Your Majesty, whatever will you do?"

"Well, really, I don't know," said the King. "There is nowhere here we can sleep for the night, and nothing we can continue our voyage in. It is a real puzzle!"

Then suddenly Mr and Mrs Noah walked up to the King and bowed stiffly, for they were made of wood.

"Your Majesties!" they said, politely. "Would you care to borrow our wooden

Ark? We can easily turn out all the animals and make it comfortable for you. It is watertight and will float very well indeed."

"I have sometimes heard of a Noah's Ark," said the King, "but I have never seen one. Let me look at it. The Queen and I are almost dry now."

So they walked out of the dolls' house and went to see the Noah's Ark. All the toys went too, and most of them were very cross with Mr and Mrs Noah.

"Fancy offering to take the King and Queen in your stupid old Ark!" they whispered to Mr Noah. "Whatever were you thinking of?"

But Mr Noah took no notice. He led the King over to the Ark, and the Queen went with Mrs Noah.

"Well!" said the King in surprise. "So that is a Noah's Ark! It looks big enough to take us all quite comfortably, much better than a small boat. It is really very kind of you, Mr Noah, to offer to lend it to us. Would you come with

us to steer it? I don't think any of my servants know how to guide an Ark."

"Certainly, certainly," said Mr Noah, blushing with delight. All the toys were most surprised, and said not a word. The King called his servants and showed them the Ark.

"Shall we get in now?" he asked.

"I must first get all the animals out," said Mr Noah. "They live there, you know, two of each kind."

Then he clapped his hands and called to the animals. They all pushed up the lid and looked out to see what was happening.

"Come out!" cried Mr Noah. "The King and Queen of Fairyland want to borrow the Ark for a little while."

Then out tumbled all the wooden animals, and walked up to the King and Queen two by two and bowed. Their Majesties were delighted, and thought they had never seen such polite animals before.

"Now, Your Majesty, I'll just borrow

a ladder from the toy farm," said Mr Noah, "and you and the Queen can climb into the Ark. Ho, soldiers, fetch some comfortable chairs from the dolls' house for Their Majesties to sit in!"

The soldiers scurried off and came back with chairs. The bear fetched the ladder from the toy farm, and Mr Noah put it against the side of the Ark. In a trice the King and Queen and all their servants were safely inside, sitting on their chairs.

Then ropes were tied to the Ark, and the soldiers hauled on them. The Ark slid across the floor and out on to the grass. Soon it was by the stream, and then, with a gentle splash, it was launched. All the toys cheered and waved goodbye. The wooden Ark animals had marched down to the water in twos, and the King and Queen laughed to see them.

Off sailed the Ark down the stream in the moonlight. It went right away to Buttercup Land, and the Prince was full of astonishment to see it.

"Thank you so much," said the King and Queen to Mr and Mrs Noah. "We don't know what we should have done without you and the wonderful Ark. Please come and see us. We will send you an invitation when we get back to Fairyland."

Mr and Mrs Noah said goodbye, and guided the Ark back home. They were simply delighted to think that they had been able to help Their Majesties. As for all the toys in the playhouse, they couldn't make enough fuss of Mr and Mrs Noah.

"We *are* sorry we laughed at the Ark," they said. "*Do* tell us all your adventures!"

And dear me, when the invitation came from the King and Queen to a moonlight party in Fairyland, for Mr and Mrs Noah and all the wooden animals, what excitement there was! And how envious all the other toys were!

Mr and Mrs Noah didn't need to go in the Ark, for the elfin messenger said he could take them by a short cut down the garden path, and along a passage in a hollow oak tree. So off they all went.

Mr and Mrs Noah went first, feeling ever so proud. Then came all the animals in twos. It really was a sight to see! I should love to have gone with them, wouldn't you?

The very strange pool

Now once upon a time Shiny-One the gnome had to take a heavy mirror to Dame Pretty. It was a very large looking-glass indeed, bigger than Shiny-One himself, so it made him puff and pant, as you can imagine.

When he got to the middle of Cuckoo Wood he felt that he really *must* have a rest. So he laid the mirror flat on the ground, with the bracken and grass peeping into it, and went to lean against a tree a little way off. And he fell fast asleep.

Now along that way came little Peep and Pry, the two naughty little boy pixies who lived at the edge of the wood. They were always peeping and prying into things that were no business of theirs — so you can guess they were most astonished to see a big flat shining thing in the middle of the wood!

"Look at that!" said Peep. "A pool!"

"A lovely, shiny pool!" said Pry. They both ran to it – and indeed, the mirror did look exactly like a shining pool of clear water, for it reflected the grass, the bracken, the trees and the sky, exactly as a sheet of water does.

"I wonder how a pool suddenly came here," said Peep. "It's really rather extraordinary. There was never one here before."

"It hasn't been raining," said Pry. "I just can't understand it. Do you suppose it is a magic pool, Peep?"

"Yes – perhaps it is," said Peep.

"Peep – shall we take a little drink from it, in case it's a wishing-pool?" whispered Pry.

"Well – do you think we'd better?" said Peep. "Suppose it belongs to somebody?"

"They'll never know," said naughty Pry. "Come on – let's scoop a little water up in our hands and drink it. We'll wish at the same time."

Peep put his hand down to the mirror – but, of course, all he felt was something hard, and not soft water!

"The pool's frozen!" he said. "Look – there's no water – only ice."

"Well, that *shows* it's magic!" said Pry at once. "That just shows it is! How could water freeze on a warm autumn day like this? It's impossible."

"I think you're right," said Peep in excitement. "Yes, I really think you are. A pool that is frozen hard on a warm day *must* be magic! Whoever it belongs to must have frozen it so that nobody could take a drink and wish."

"Ah – but we can manage to trick the owner!" said Pry in a whisper. "We can break the ice, Peep – and drink the water below! Can't we?"

"Of course!" said Peep. "Come on – let's break it and drink quickly, before anyone comes."

So they took stones and banged the pool hard – crack! The mirror broke into little pieces – and to the pixies' great astonishment there was no water underneath!

"Stranger and stranger!" said Peep. "I wish there was somebody we could tell this to."

Then they saw Shiny-One, the gnome, not very far off. He was just waking up. They ran to him.

"I say, there's a magic pool over there!" said Peep.

"We knew it was magic, because it was frozen hard," added Pry. "So we cracked the ice to get a drink of the water underneath – but there wasn't any! Did you ever know such magic?"

"What nonsense are you talking?" said Shiny-One crossly. He knew Peep and Pry well and didn't like the way they poked their noses into things that had nothing to do with them. "A magic pool – frozen on a day like this! Rubbish!"

Peep and Pry took him to the pool – and Shiny-One stared down in horror at his poor broken mirror.

"My mirror!" he said. "The one I was selling to Dame Pretty. Look what you've done, with your silly interfering ways – smashed that beautiful big mirror! You bad pixies! How much money have you got in your pockets? You'll have to pay for that mirror!"

Peep and Pry tried to run away – but Shiny-One caught hold of them both. He turned them upside down and shook them well. All their money rolled out of their pockets.

"Thank you," said Shiny-One, and he turned the pixies the right way up. "Thank you! Just enough to pay for a new mirror, I think. Now run off before I think of smacking you both."

Peep and Pry ran off, crying. Shiny-One dug a hole with a stick and buried all the bits of broken mirror, so that nobody's feet would get cut.

As for poor Peep and Pry, they had to go without buying sweets for four weeks, because all their money had gone – so maybe they won't go poking their noses about quite so much another time!

Peter's busy afternoon

"**M**ummy! Where are you?" cried Peter, rushing at top speed into the kitchen.

"Peter, don't make me jump like that," said his mother, almost dropping the tin of cakes she was taking out of the oven.

"Oooh, Mummy – may I have one of those buns?" said Peter at once. His mother looked at him.

"Did you post my letter for me this morning?" she asked him. Peter put his hand in his pocket and drew out a letter, going rather red as he looked at it.

"Blow – no, I didn't. Sorry, I'll post it now. Then may I have a bun?"

"No," said his mother. "Give me the

letter. I'll ask the milkman to post it. I'm afraid you can't have a bun, as you haven't even bothered to do this little thing for me."

Peter sulked. He kicked the leg of the table. "Stop doing that," said his mother. "What was it you wanted to ask me when you came rushing in, Peter?"

Peter cheered up. "Oh, Mummy –

could you give me some money, please? There are some simply wonderful pistols in the toy shop. They go BANG like anything."

"Why should I give you any money?" asked his mother, setting the buns to cool on a tray. "Why should you expect anyone to do things for you and give you things when you never, never do anything for anyone else?"

"Oh! I *do*," said Peter, indignantly.

"Did you tidy out the shed for Daddy when he asked you?" said his mother.

"No, I forgot," said Peter.

"Did you mend your little sister's brick box when you had broken the lid?" asked his mother.

"No," said Peter, sulkily.

"Did you post my letter? Did you fetch me the meat? Did you remember to shut the back gate? Did you pick up your coat from the floor?" asked his mother.

"No, I suppose I didn't," said Peter, and kicked the leg of the table again.

"Well, then – why should you expect

me to please you and hand out money to you, if you don't do anything for anyone else?" said his mother. "No, Peter. You can't have the money. I feel ashamed of you. Go away, please. I don't really feel I want to talk to you any more."

"Well, you *might*," said Peter, looking hurt. "Eileen's in bed with a cold – I do think you might let me be with you as I can't be with her."

"It isn't much of a cold," said his mother. "You *could* be with her if you wanted to. She would love you to read to her because she's too little to read herself."

"I suppose I'd better go up then," said Peter, unwillingly.

"No. She's asleep now," said his mother. "And I have asked Ronnie to come and be with her this afternoon. He's always so nice with the little ones. She won't want you."

Peter kicked his way out of the kitchen, scuffling his shoes on the floor as he went. He went and sat down in the shed, looking gloomy.

He didn't like his mother saying she didn't want him with her. He didn't like Ronnie being asked to read to Eileen. He felt left out.

Then he began to be a little more sensible. It was his own fault. He never remembered to do a single thing he was told! No wonder his mother said she didn't want to talk to him.

He kicked his heels against the box he was sitting on. He thought of Ronnie reading to Eileen. He was fond of his gentle little sister and he didn't want somebody else taking his place. He was fond of his mother, too. "Yes, I am, though nobody would think it!" he said to himself, kicking the box harder and harder. "Blow! I'd better turn over a new leaf. The thing is – can I? New leaves are jolly hard to turn over!"

When he saw Ronnie going up the stairs to play with Eileen that afternoon he felt rather upset. He must begin the leaf-turning as soon as possible! He belonged to a nice family and it wouldn't do to be the only nasty one in it. Daddy was always unselfish and generous as well as his mother.

He went to the shed and tidied it thoroughly. It looked very nice when he had finished it. Then he took out his mother's bicycle and cleaned it. It did look lovely when it was done. "And I shan't let Mummy pay me for doing it, like she did last time," he thought. "I'll do it for nothing, just to show her I'm not always selfish and forgetful."

He saw Wags the dog and gave him a good brushing. He remembered that the back gate wanted a nail under the latch to make it work properly, and he went and hammered one in. He began to have a very nice feeling inside him, indeed.

"Now what can I do for Eileen?" he thought. "I simply must do something, so that she'll know *I* was thinking of her while Ronnie was reading to her."

He went to Eileen's little garden. He knew she wanted to plant some flower seeds there. She was saving up to buy them. Her garden was full of weeds and wanted digging over.

Peter didn't like digging. He screwed up his nose and wondered if he would tackle it. Yes, he would. So he went to get a spade and a basket.

He weeded the whole of the little garden, and then he took the spade and began to dig.

It was hard work. He dug and he dug and he dug. He had to take off his coat. Then he had to take off his jersey and dig in his shirt-sleeves! Gracious, who would have thought that a little garden like that needed so much digging?

Wouldn't Eileen be pleased! My word, she'd be very, very surprised when she saw how nice her garden looked. What a pity she hadn't got enough money to buy her seeds the very next day and plant them now the garden was ready!

Peter wished he had some money, then he could buy her some. But he hadn't even a penny.

He was just digging the very last bit of all when his spade turned up something that shone. He bent down and picked it up. He rubbed the wet earth from it – and what *do* you think it was!

"A shining, silvery coin!" cried Peter. "What a find! How in the world did it get here?"

And then he remembered. "Of course! Eileen had some money on her birthday, and she lost it when she went to water her garden that evening. And it must have dropped out of her pocket then, and got buried – and here it is!"

Peter was as pleased as if it had been his own money! He raced indoors with it. He actually remembered to scrape his shoes and wipe them well. He ran up the stairs.

"Eileen! Oh, hallo, Ronnie! I say, Eileen – I was digging up your garden just now – and I found the money you lost on your birthday. Look! Now you can buy all the seeds you want – and your garden is ready to plant them in!"

"Peter! Why, how marvellous!" cried Eileen, her face going red with delight. "My own money! And what a lot of money! I'll buy my seeds tomorrow, if Mummy lets me go out. I'm much better now. Thank you, Peter, *thank* you, for doing my garden. It was most awfully kind of you!"

Daddy and Mother were told about the bit of good luck. Mother smiled at Peter. "Who cleaned my bicycle?" she said.

"I did," said Peter. "For nothing – just to make up a bit, you know, for the things I forgot."

"Who tidied the shed for me?" asked Daddy.

"I did – and that was for nothing, too," said Peter.

"Who mended the back gate?" asked

Mother. "And who brushed Wags? He looks so nice."

"Well, I did," said Peter, rubbing his nose as he always did when he felt a bit awkward. "I know I'm pretty awful most times, Mummy – but honestly, I'm turning over a new leaf at the moment. And please don't think I did it just to get that pistol, because I didn't."

"I don't think that, dear," said his mother, and she kissed him.

Now, the next day, Eileen went out with her birthday money and the money she had already saved, and bought her seeds. Then she marched off to the toy shop. Can you guess what she bought? Yes, she bought that pistol.

She walked home with it proudly. She showed it to her mother, and made it go off BANG!

Peter heard it and came rushing in. "Oh! You lucky, lucky girl, you've got the pistol I've been longing for! Did you buy it out of the birthday money?"

"Yes," said Eileen. "I had some over.

So I bought it. Isn't it fine?"

"Rather! Will you lend it to me just *some*times?" said Peter, longingly.

"No. I'll *give* it to you," said Eileen, with a laugh. "Why, I *bought* it for you, silly! *I* don't want a pistol. Here you are, Peter. If you hadn't dug my garden you wouldn't have found my birthday money, and I wouldn't have been able to buy my seeds to plant today. And I wouldn't have had any money over to buy your pistol!"

Well, what do you think of that? Peter was so pleased that he let out a tremendous whoop of joy, which made Wags jump almost out of his skin.

"Oh, *thanks*! I say, isn't it super? BANG, BANG, BANG! Oh, Mummy, does it make you jump? I promise I won't shoot it in the house."

"Thank you, Peter," said his mother. "And as you've turned over a new leaf, I can depend on your promise, can't I? Well – I'm very, very glad you got your pistol."

Billy-up-the-tree

"**B**illy! If I catch you climbing trees again I'll send you straight to bed!" said his mother. "Look at your shorts – torn to bits! And you've got a most enormous hole in that new jersey. It's very naughty of you."

"The other boys climb trees," said Billy, looking sulky.

"The other boys are bigger, they're more careful, and they only climb when they have their oldest clothes on," said his mother. "You may fall – and if you do you'll break an arm or a leg, and feel very sorry for yourself indeed. I forbid you to climb trees until you are older."

Well, that was that. Billy was cross and upset. But he didn't like to disobey.

Daddy didn't like boys who disobeyed their mothers. In fact, he was very stern about it indeed!

Now, a week later, Billy was out in the garden by himself. Tom looked over the wall and grinned.

"Hallo! I've been tree-climbing. I got right to the top of a big chestnut. I bet you've never climbed a big tree."

"I have, then," said Billy. "We've got a chestnut in our garden. I've climbed that."

"Not to the top," said Tom. "I bet you wouldn't dare."

"I would, then," said Billy. "But I've been forbidden to. And, anyway, I haven't got my old clothes on."

"You're just making excuses," said Tom, and he laughed. "You daren't climb up that tree!"

"All right. You just see, then!" said Billy, and he ran to the chestnut tree. Up he went, branch by branch, for the tree was not very difficult to climb. Then – oh, dear! – he caught his coat

94

on a sharp piece, and tore it. Bother! Now Mummy would be cross again.

"Go on – up to the top," said Tom, sitting on the wall and watching. "That's it. Go right up!"

And soon Billy *was* at the top of the chestnut tree and could see a very long way indeed. He could see right over the tops of the houses, and as far as the river. The wind blew and the tree swayed a little. Billy felt as if he was on a ship at sea.

"Somebody's coming! I'm going," said Tom, and disappeared. Billy looked down between the branches. He couldn't see anyone – but he could hear somebody whistling. Goodness – it was Daddy! How dreadful if he was seen.

He sat quite still. After a while Daddy went indoors again. Then Billy began to climb down the tree. But after going down two or three branches he stopped.

"This isn't the way I came up," he said to himself. "I can't get down this way."

He climbed up again, and then started

down a different way. But somehow or other he couldn't get down. No matter how he tried, he couldn't seem to get past one of the branches. His coat stuck again, and another hole was made. Then his shorts caught, and that meant another tear.

Billy began to feel afraid. Suppose he never could get down that tree! He must. He simply must. So he tried again, but it wasn't a bit of good. Either he came to a branch that was right in his way or else he came to such a big drop that he was afraid to try it.

He sat in a fork of the tree and wondered what to do. "I daren't call out for help. If Mummy or Daddy know I've been climbing again they really will be angry. I wouldn't be surprised if Daddy sends me to bed. Oh, *how* can I get down?"

Well, he couldn't. He just couldn't. And he didn't dare to call for help either. So he sat up there till tea-time. He heard his mother calling him, but he didn't dare to answer. He went without his tea. He began to feel very bored and miserable, and very hungry, too.

"Why did I climb this silly tree just to show Tom I could? It's all his fault! How long have I got to stay here?"

It grew cold and Billy shivered. Then, to his horror, it began to grow dark as well. It was evening.

His mother called again. His father came out into the garden to look for him. There he was, almost under the tree, and Billy didn't dare to say a word.

But he couldn't stay there all night, he really couldn't! He began to try to climb down again. Then he got stuck, and couldn't go up or down. The wind got up, and the tree shook.

"It's terribly, terribly cold," said Billy to himself, trying to pull his coat round him. "Oooh! How the wind blows! The tree is rocking just like a ship. I hope I shan't fall out – though perhaps that's the only way I'll ever get out of this horrible tree!"

By now his mother and father were really worried about Billy. Wherever could he be? Ought they to ring up the police? They couldn't think *what* to do. Billy never, never missed his tea – and now it was almost supper-time.

Then they heard a miserable voice calling, "Mummy! Daddy! Help me, help me!"

"That's Billy!" said his mother, clutching his father. "His voice comes from the garden. Where can he be?"

They ran out and listened. "Where are you, Billy? Where are you?" called his mother.

"Here, Mummy, here! Up in the chestnut tree," called Billy, miserably. "And I can't get down. I've been here for hours and hours. What shall I do?"

"Up the tree! And you were forbidden to climb!" said Daddy's voice. "How far up are you?"

"Almost at the top," said Billy. "And I'm so cold."

"I'll get a ladder," said Daddy. Billy

was so glad to hear that. Of course – a ladder! He hadn't thought of that. He had been worrying and worrying how he was ever to get down.

Daddy fetched the ladder. He put it up against the tree, running it between the broad, spreading branches. The tip of it reached Billy's feet.

He began to climb down. "Now, be careful!" called his father. "It's dark. Go slowly."

Billy's hands were so cold and his feet so icy that he could hardly feel the rungs of the ladder. And quite suddenly he slipped and fell. His father tried to catch him, but couldn't. Then a dreadful pain ran through Billy's leg and he yelled out. "I'm hurt! My leg, oh, my leg!"

Yes, his poor leg was broken. The doctor had to come and set it, and Billy was so frightened and upset that he couldn't help crying.

"No football for you for some time, old son," said the doctor. "No games at all!"

He went, and Mummy and Daddy

came to sit beside him. Billy told them all about it – how he had climbed because of what Tom said – and then had been too afraid to call for help – and had got so very, very cold.

"Now you'll punish me, and that will make me feel worse than ever," said Billy.

"We don't punish people who have punished themselves much harder than we would ever have punished them," said Daddy. "No football – no games of any sort – that is a dreadful punishment for someone who is so good at them. We are as sad as you are, Billy. We had so much looked forward to seeing you play in football matches."

"I've spoilt everything," said Billy. "I'm sorry. And how Tom will laugh!"

But Tom didn't. He was upset, too, and he came every day to sit with Billy, and he helped him to walk, too, when his leg was put into plaster.

Now Billy's leg is all right again, and he is running about as fast as ever.

And today his mother told him he could climb trees – he really was quite big enough.

"But never climb one you can't get down!" she said. "And if you do, then yell for help!"

But somehow poor Billy doesn't want to climb trees any more. What a shame!

Silly Simon and the goat

Simon had had a cold, and his ears had ached. He had been very miserable. Now he was better, and up again, but he was rather deaf. That was horrid.

"You'll be able to go to school again tomorrow," said his mother. "That will be nice for you. Today you shall stay at home and help me."

So Simon helped his mother. He fetched in the washing from the line. He ran to the grocer's to get the butter, and he took the baby out for a little walk. He really was a great help.

"You have been quite a sensible boy for once," said his mother, pleased. Silly Simon wasn't always sensible.

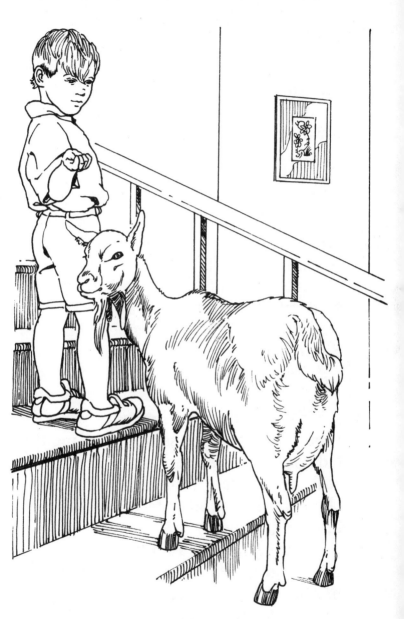

He sometimes did very silly things, and then his mother was cross.

He was pleased. "Well, Mother, you always think I haven't got brains," he said. "But I have. I'm really a very clever boy."

"Well, I hope you go on being a clever boy for the rest of the day," said his mother. "Now, I'm going upstairs to have a little rest. Baby is fast asleep."

She went upstairs, and then she remembered that she wanted her old coat to mend. So she called down to Simon.

"Simon! Fetch me the old coat, will you?"

Simon didn't hear her very well. He thought his mother said, "Fetch me the old goat." He was rather surprised, but still, as he was feeling very good and obedient, he set off to fetch the old goat in from the field.

He caught him, and led him to the house on a rope. He called up to his mother. "I've got it for you."

"Well, bring it upstairs, and hang it over the banisters," called his mother. Simon felt more astonished than before. It was funny to want the old goat brought into the house, but still stranger to want it upstairs hung over the banisters.

"The goat won't like it!" he called up after a bit. His mother was now lying down, half-asleep, and she only half-heard what he said.

"Don't be silly!" she said. "It won't hurt the coat. But hang it in the hall, if you'd rather."

"Hang you in the hall?" said Simon to the surprised goat. "Which would you rather, Goat? I can hang you in the hall, or take you upstairs and put you over the banisters."

The goat didn't seem to mind which. So Simon took it into the hall, and looked at the pegs there. He tried to tie the rope to a peg, but the goat broke away at once, pulling the peg-rack down with a crash.

"Simon!" shouted his mother crossly. "What in the world are you doing? Be quiet."

"There!" said Simon to the goat. "You'll be getting into trouble if you make noises like that. You'd better come upstairs. I think it would be easier to put you over the banisters, after all."

So the goat was dragged upstairs. It made a great noise and Simon's mother called out again.

"You'll wake the baby next! What are you making all that noise for?"

"I'm dragging the goat up," panted Simon. "It won't come."

"A coat isn't as heavy as all that," said his mother crossly. "What a fuss you make to be sure! I hope you're not dragging it on the floor."

Simon at last got the goat to the top of the stairs. He tried to get it across the banisters, but the goat simply wouldn't go. As fast as Simon lifted it up one end, it slipped to the ground the other end. It was a most annoying goat.

"Simon! Whatever are you doing out there?" called his mother. "I shall get up in a minute and punish you."

"There!" said Simon to the goat fiercely. "You'll get me into trouble if you don't behave. Now, just you let me put you across the banisters!"

But it was no good. The goat wouldn't be at all helpful. It clattered with its four feet, it slid here and there, and was altogether most obstinate.

It suddenly got very tired of Simon. It backed a little way, put its head down, ran at Simon and caught him full on its head. It butted him hard, and Simon rose in the air with a yell, sailed down the stairs, and landed at the bottom with a crash. He howled loudly. The baby woke up and yelled, too.

The bed creaked as Simon's mother leapt out. She flung open the door to glare at Simon – but instead she found herself glaring at the old goat, who glared back, and looked as if he might butt her at any moment. Simon's mother hurriedly stepped back into the bedroom and shut the door.

She called through it. "You bad boy, Simon! How dare you bring that old goat up here? Take him back to the field at once!"

"Well, you *told* me to bring him here and hang him over the banisters," wailed Simon. "You did, you did!"

"Oh! Oh, you foolish, silly, stupid boy!" cried his mother. "I told you to fetch my old *coat* – I wanted to mend it! Oh, why did I ever say you were good and sensible today?"

The goat trotted neatly downstairs and into the hall. It went into the kitchen and out of the back door. It had had enough of Simon and Simon's mother and the crying baby.

"It's gone!" said Simon. "But, oh, Mother, it's taken a rug with it to eat!"

"Oh, *has* it!" cried his mother, and shot out of her bedroom and downstairs to catch the goat. But she was too late. The goat had eaten the rug.

Then Simon got sent up to his room, and he was very upset about it.

"I try to be good and sensible and obedient and this is what I get for it!" he wept. "I'll never try again."

"Well, if you do things like that when you are trying to be good, you'd better stop!" said his mother.

Poor Simon! You wouldn't think anyone would be so silly, would you?

The boy who kicked

Nobody liked to sit next to Reggie at school, because he used to kick. He thought it was funny to kick the children beside him, or behind him, too, if he could.

But they didn't think it was funny, because Reggie wore big boots, and the kicks hurt. He was a big boy for his age, so nobody liked to kick him back. He could always kick much harder!

He kicked dogs if he could. The cats got out of his way quickly. If he couldn't kick anything else, he kicked stones along the road, and he was so pleased if they hit anyone!

Once he kicked his mother. But when his father heard about it, he punished

Reggie so severely that he decided he would never do that again. His father made him take off his boots, as soon as he came inside the house, for two weeks. So Reggie thought he would keep his kicks for outside. It was more fun to kick people or animals that couldn't punish him for it!

One day he went along the lane, going home from school. He came across a limping dog, and he kicked it. The dog yelped, but he couldn't run away because he had a thorn in his foot. So Reggie kicked him again.

"Stop that!" said a sharp voice, and Reggie saw a small man, not any bigger than himself, looking at him from the hedge.

"Pooh!" said Reggie, and kicked out again.

The man jumped down and held Reggie hard. Reggie kicked at the man's ankles and made him yell. "You let me go!" said Reggie.

"I don't believe you're a boy at all,"

said the man. "I believe you're a little donkey, who has been changed by a spell into a little boy. Poor thing! I'm sorry for you."

Reggie kicked at a flower and its head flew off. "Don't be silly," he said to the man.

"I'll change you back to a donkey," said the man. "I've often changed people back to their own shape when witches or wizards had turned them into something. And I can easily turn you back into yourself, poor little kicking donkey."

And before Reggie knew what was happening, the little man was drawing a circle in white chalk round him, and was chanting some very strange words indeed.

When he had finished, there was no Reggie there. Instead there was a nice little grey donkey, with long ears and a tail that switched from side to side.

"There!" said the little man, and patted the donkey. "You're back to

your own shape, little kicker. You will
be happy now. Donkeys always kick,
and people expect them to. But not little
boys."

Reggie was so angry that he kicked
out with his hind legs at once. But
the little man skipped nimbly out of

113

the way. "Good little donkey!" he said. "Good little kicker!"

Reggie went slowly home, angry and frightened. He found himself munching grass and thistles. *Thistles!* He didn't want to eat them at all, but he had to, because he was a donkey.

A man came up to him. "Where are you straying from?" he asked. "You'd better come with me. You must belong to the farmer near by."

Reggie kicked out at once, because he didn't like the man. "Oho!" said the fellow at once. "Bad-tempered, are you? Well, I've a cure for that!" And he quickly put a rope around Reggie's neck and tried to lead him away.

Reggie broke away from him and trotted home. His mother was amazed to see a little grey donkey putting his head round the kitchen door. "Go away!" she said. "Do you belong to the milkman? Go away."

It was dreadful to have his own mother telling him to go away. The milkman came just then, and Reggie's mother asked him to take the donkey out to the lane. "He must have wandered away from somewhere," she said.

Reggie didn't want to go. He kicked out at the milkman. The man, who was used to donkeys, gave him a sharp slap. "A kicker, are you?" he said. "Kickers are no use to anyone. Out you go!"

Into the lane went poor Reggie, and the milkman shut the gate so that he could not go in to see his mother again.

He spent the whole afternoon out, and he didn't like it a bit. In the evening the little magic man came again.

"I say!" he said. "I find I've made a mistake. You really *ought* to be a little boy, not a donkey. But you can't blame me for my mistake, because of your kicking. I'd better change you back."

"Please do," hee-hawed Reggie.

"Well, I will – but be careful you don't get changed into a donkey by one of my friends, if you start kicking again," said the little fellow. "They'll think the same as I did – that you're a donkey changed by a witch into a nasty little boy!"

Once more the chalk circle was drawn round Reggie, and the magic words chanted. Then, hey presto! he was himself again, with no long ears to twitch, nor long tail to swing. How glad he was!

His father was angry with him for staying out all afternoon, and wouldn't believe him when he told him what had happened. "If I have any more nonsense from you, I shall send you to bed," he said. "How would you like that?"

Reggie knew he wouldn't like it at all, so he said nothing. He didn't even want to kick! He didn't feel like a kicking donkey any more, and never would.

Now it's quite safe to sit next to Reggie at school, and not even the slowest old dog is afraid of him. It's a good thing that little man found out his mistake, or Reggie would still be in a field somewhere, munching thistles!

Pink! Pink!

Hey-Presto, the wizard, had a wonderful cloak. Whenever he swung it round his shoulders he disappeared at once, because it had very powerful magic in it.

The cloak was most useful to the wizard. He wore it whenever he wanted to be invisible, and then he was able to do all kinds of things.

He could slip into other wizards' castles and watch them at their magic work without being seen. He could go into Witch Green-Eyes' cottage and stand unseen beside her as she stirred spells into her big black pot. He could swing his cloak round him when visitors came that he didn't want to bother about. Nobody could see him then!

"A most useful cloak!" said Hey-Presto, whenever he hung it up in his cupboard, and locked the door. "An invaluable cloak! I couldn't do without it. I must never, never let my enemies get it."

One day when he took it out of the cupboard, Miggy, his old servant, saw it.

"Good gracious, Master!" she said. "How *can* you wear that dirty old cloak? What colour is it meant to be? It's so dirty that I can't even tell if it's blue, red or green!"

"It's pink," said the wizard, looking at it. "At least, it's *supposed* to be pink! It *does* look dirty, doesn't it? Well, well – I suppose I've used it for over a hundred years now – no wonder it is dirty!"

"It's smelly, too," said Miggy, wrinkling her nose. "Pooh! It needs washing, Master. Fancy using a thing for over a hundred years and not having it washed. And look at this hole!"

"Dear me, yes," said the wizard, quite alarmed. "It won't do to get big holes in it – bits of me will be seen then, through the holes. Whatever shall I do?"

"I'll wash and mend it," said Miggy, firmly.

"It's too precious," said Hey-Presto, clutching it tightly.

"Now listen," said Miggy, "that cloak smells so dirty that very soon people will know you are near them, even though you're invisible. You let me wash it. I'll be very, very careful."

"All right, Miggy. But when you hang it out to dry, please put up a clothes line in the walled garden and make sure the gate is locked," said Hey-Presto. "If anyone saw this cloak on the line they might steal it!"

"Oh, Master, I'll be as careful of your cloak as if it was made of gold!" said old Miggy, putting it over her arm. "My word – what a horrible smell! It must be *five* hundred years old, not one!"

She went off and got a tub full of

boiling water. In went the magic cloak, and Miggy scrubbed it up and down in the suds.

"Just look at the dirt coming out," said Miggy, in disgust. "Why, there's more dirt than cloak! I'll have to wash it three or four times before it's really clean."

When she had finished washing it, she could hardly believe her eyes! The cloak was pink – the loveliest pink imaginable!

Miggy shook it out and then called her master. "Master, come here! Did you ever see such a lovely colour in your life?"

Hey-Presto looked at his cloak. Why, it didn't seem the same one! "It's the colour of almond blossom!" he said. "It's the colour of wild roses in the hedge! And yes – it's exactly the colour of the sky when it's pink at sunset time!"

"Yes," said Miggy. "Shame on you for wearing it so dirty! I'm going to hang it out to dry and then I'll mend it for you."

"In the walled garden, mind!" called the wizard, anxiously. "Nobody can get in there, nobody at all."

Miggy hurried into the walled garden. She had already put up a washing line there. She went to the door in the wall and locked it carefully, putting the key into her pocket. Now nobody could get into the garden from outside, and the walls were far too high to climb.

She looked at the clouds racing across the sky. "Nice windy day – the cloak will dry quickly!" she thought. "I'll press it tonight and mend it – and I'll see that the master doesn't get it so dirty again. It shan't go for more than twenty years this time before it's washed again."

She pegged the cloak carefully on the line and watched it flapping in the wind. It would soon be dry!

"I'll fetch it about three o'clock," she thought and trotted indoors. She kept an eye on it through the kitchen window, and was pleased to see that it was drying nicely.

At three o'clock she went into the garden to unpeg the cloak – but it wasn't there! The line was empty – and three or four clothes pegs lay scattered on the ground!

Miggy gave a scream that brought Hey-Presto out at once. "MASTER! MASTER! Your cloak's been stolen!"

Hey-Presto came at top speed. He saw the empty washing line and the scattered pegs and he groaned. He ran to the garden door that led out into the lane, but it was locked. No one could have got in that way.

"I kept that cloak under my eye the whole time," sobbed Miggy. "I looked out from the kitchen window almost every minute. Nobody could have got in without my seeing them, nobody! They couldn't get out without being seen either."

"Oh, yes they could," said Hey-Presto, grimly. "All the thief had to do was to swing the cloak round his shoulders and he and the cloak too would be invisible at once. He could go where he liked then – even creep in past you through the kitchen, out into the hall and walk out of the front door. Nobody would see him. What *am* I to do? My wonderful cloak! I MUST get it back!"

"The thief won't always be wearing it, sir, and it's such a bright, glowing pink that it would be very easy to recognize it," said poor Miggy, very upset indeed. "Can't you offer a reward, Master, to anyone – even to any animal or bird – who finds it or brings news of it?"

"Yes. Yes, I'll certainly do that," said Hey-Presto. Immediately he sent out hundreds of little pixie heralds, complete with trumpets, to announce his loss and the reward for finding the cloak.

Everyone was excited. The country was searched from top to bottom. But no news came in. Nobody had ever seen the cloak, hardly anyone had even known of it – so how *could* it have been stolen?

Rabbits searched down burrows. Fish

in the rivers hunted here and there. Owls looked in hollow trees, swallows looked in barns. It was no good – nobody saw anything pink that was big enough to be the cloak.

And then one day a chaffinch flew down to Miggy in great excitement. "Pink!" he called loudly. "PINK-PINK!"

"What do you mean? Have you found the pink cloak?" cried Miggy. "Where is it?"

"Pink-pink-pink!" shouted the little chaffinch, fluffing out his pretty chest. "PINK!"

"I'll come with you," said Miggy, putting on her bonnet. "Lead the way, Chaffinch. I'm sure you think you've found the cloak!"

"Chip-chip-chip-chip, cherry-erry-erry, chippy, HERE-WE-ARE!" sang the chaffinch, flying up into a tall tree just outside the walled garden. And there, caught on a high branch, and wrapped round and round it, was the magic cloak, as pink as ever, but a little dirty.

"Yes! You're right! It *is* the cloak!" cried Miggy. "You clever bird, you VERY clever bird! Wait here till I get a ladder, and don't you DARE to tell anyone else!"

She fetched a long ladder and up and up she went. She unwrapped the cloak from the branch and slipped it round her so that she might use both her hands to climb down the ladder again. At once, to the chaffinch's astonishment, she vanished and the cloak vanished, too!

"Pink!" he called anxiously. Miggy's voice answered him from the ladder.

"It's all right. I'm still here, climbing down the ladder. Wearing the cloak is the easiest way for me to carry it!"

She ran to the wizard, taking the cloak off just as she got to him. "Master! It's found! Here it is!"

"Where was it?" asked Hey-Presto, startled and delighted.

"Caught up in a tree not far from the walled garden!" said Miggy. "Nobody stole it! The strong wind must have blown it off the line straight up into the tree, and wrapped it round a branch – and there it's been ever since!"

"But who found it?" asked Hey-Presto, looking to see if the cloak was damaged.

"The chaffinch who nests in that tree," said Miggy. "He came and told me. He was so excited he could only say, 'Pink! Pink!' But I guessed what he meant, of course."

"Then he must have the reward," said Hey-Presto. "Call him here, the clever bird."

The chaffinch came. He flew in at the window, calling, "Pink! Pink!"

"There! He can't say anything but that at the moment," said Miggy. "He's been shouting out the news to everyone – he's so proud of himself!"

"Chaffinch, you have earned the reward," said Hey-Presto, and the little bird flew on to his shoulder. "You may have a sack of gold – a box of spells – or anything else you can think of."

The chaffinch whispered a little song into the wizard's ear. Hey-Presto laughed.

"What does he want for a reward?" asked Miggy.

"Nothing! He says money is no use to him – and he's frightened of spells – and as he has a nest of his own, with a dear little wife and four beautiful nestlings, he has got everything he can possibly want," said the wizard. "He just wants to know if he can go on telling everyone that he found my pink cloak – he's so very, very proud of that."

"Well, let him," said Miggy. "It's a reward that won't cost you a penny – and he'll be glad that he and all his family can boast about finding your magic cloak. People love boasting – even birds do!"

"You're right," said Hey-Presto, and he turned to the excited little chaffinch. He spoke very solemnly.

"As your reward for finding my pink

cloak you may tell everyone in the world!" he said. "You may shout the news at the top of your voice year after year!"

And, believe it or not, from that day to this every chaffinch shouts out the news each spring and summer. You *must* listen, you really must.

"Pink!" he calls loudly. "PINK, PINK, PINK!"

Listen for him, will you, and call out, "Clever bird! Who found the magic cloak? What colour was it?"

And he will put his knowing little head on one side and answer you at once.

"Pink! PINK-PINK-PINK!"

How John got his ducklings

John and his sister Mary liked playing on their uncle's farm next door. Best of all they liked the baby animals and birds. John was always wanting some for his very, very own. But his Uncle Tom wouldn't let him have any.

"No, John," he said. "You'd forget to feed them or something. Wait till you're old enough."

"But, Uncle, I'm old enough now," said John. "I would feed them and water them well, and Mary would help me. Just let me have two or three yellow chicks for my own, or some of those little yellow ducks. *Do*, Uncle." But Uncle Tom shook his head, and John knew it was no use saying any more.

So he contented himself with trying to help feed the animals, and running after Jim, the yardman, when he went to make the pig-meal or hen food. But he longed to have something that was really and truly his own.

One day Jim went to cart hay for the barn. John and Mary thought they would cart hay too. John had a little wooden cart and wooden horse. He could fill the cart with hay and then pull it along by dragging the horse after him. Mary would help him to put the hay in the barn just like Jim was doing.

So he piled hay into his wooden cart. When John had filled the cart he picked up the string tied to his wooden horse's head and he and Mary pulled it. But dear me, the horse caught its wooden stand against a stone and the front wheel fell off.

"Oh!" said John, in dismay. "It's broken! Poor old Dobbin! I'll take you to Jim. Perhaps he can mend you for me tonight."

He took the horse from the cart and ran off to find Jim, while Mary wheeled the cartful of hay into a hedge nearby.

"Yes, I'll mend it for you sometime," said Jim. "But not tonight, and not while we're haymaking."

He took the horse from John. By that time it was dinner-time, and he and Mary had to run home to wash. John forgot all about the cartful of hay.

It stayed there quite forgotten until one fine morning when a big white duck found the cart under the hedge. Summer flowers had grown over it and it was very hard to see.

When she spied the hay inside, she climbed into the cart very clumsily and sat down. What a fine place to lay an egg! She laid a beautiful big greeny-grey egg there and then sat on it for a while before she went back to the pond.

Each day the duck came to the little wooden cart and stood under the hedge, and laid a nice big egg there. Soon there were twelve, and the duck looked at them proudly.

She made up her mind to sit on them and keep them warm. She just fitted the wooden cart nicely, and she liked the hay inside because it made such a nice soft nest for her eggs.

John waited and waited for Jim to mend his little wooden horse – and after some weeks Jim did mend it. Then John and Mary had to hunt for John's wooden cart! They had forgotten where they had left it. Nobody had seen it, and it was a puzzle where to look for it.

"John!" called his uncle. "You might look out for ducks' eggs while you're hunting for your cart. I think one of the ducks has been laying away each day, and she may have a nest somewhere."

"I'll look hard," said John.

"You can have the eggs for yourself if you find them," said Uncle Tom.

Oooh! If only John and Mary could find them! But they knew how clever ducks were at laying eggs in places they couldn't find or couldn't get at, so they hadn't much hope of finding them.

Suddenly John remembered where he had left his wooden cart. Of course! He had been carting hay like Jim when his horse had broken. Mary must have left his cart under the hedge with the hay.

Sure enough there was his little wooden cart under the hedge, just where Mary had put it all those weeks ago.

John and Mary ran to it – and a big, fat, white duck flew off the cart, leaving behind a nest of beautiful eggs!

John fitted his horse into the shafts and trotted across the farmyard to where Uncle was working.

"Look!" called John. "She's got a whole lot of eggs! Can I have them? I should think they will soon hatch into ducklings!"

"Well, well!" said Uncle Tom, smiling. "Yes, you can have them, John, since you found them."

One day the eggs hatched into yellow ducklings, twelve of them! They follow John everywhere around the farm.

Does he look after them well? Of course he does!

"I shall always love ducklings best," John says, "because they were the first things I had for my *very* own. And I'll never give my little wooden cart away, because it was there I found the eggs!"

Will and Won't

There were once two brothers. One was called William and the other was called Walter. But their mother said they ought to have been named Will and Won't!

Will would always do anything he was asked, and he did it cheerfully and with a smile. Walter wouldn't. He sulked or sighed or grumbled when his mother asked him to run any errand or do any little job.

"Will always says, 'Yes, I will,' but Walter won't do a thing!" said their mother. "Will and Won't, that's what they are – Will and Won't!"

And, dear me, that's what everyone began to call them. "We'll ask Will," said

the girls, when they had lost a ball up
on the roof. "He'll get it for us. No good
asking Won't. He won't do a thing for
anyone!"

Now, one day the boys' mother badly
wanted an errand run to the lady who
did her washing for her. She lived right
at the other end of the town.

"Dear me," thought Mummy. "I
hardly like to ask Will to go – he's
already got wood in for me this morning,
and cleaned out the shed, and run to

139

the grocer's. It doesn't seem fair to ask him to do any more – especially as he's settled down to read his book."

So she called Won't. "Won't! Come here a minute, will you?"

"What for?" called back Won't, rudely.

"You come and see!" said his mother, and Won't had to go. "I want you to go to the lady who does the washing for us," said Mummy. "She said she would have your clean shirts ready for me today."

"Mummy, I can't go all that way!" said Won't, sulkily. "I really can't. Get Will to go."

"He's already done a lot of jobs for me," said Won't's mother, sharply. "It's your turn to do something."

"Always having to do jobs and errands!" grumbled Won't, scowling and making his face very ugly. "Can't a boy have any peace?"

"Look here, my boy, when you belong to a family, you don't only take all the good things, you share in the bothersome ones, too, and you help out when you can," said his mother. "If you don't do that you don't deserve to have a mother to look after you, and a father to work for you! Take-All and Do-Nothing, that's what you are! Now, you turn over a new leaf and do things with a smile, as Will does!"

Won't turned away sulkily. He wanted to finish his jigsaw. It seemed very important to him. He sat down just to see if he could finish it quickly. And, of course, he forgot all about what his mother wanted him to do!

"Won't! You haven't been for our clean shirts," said Will suddenly. "Mummy *will* be upset. She badly wanted our clean shirts for tomorrow."

"Bother! I forgot!" said Won't. "Oh, Will, you go – you know the way better than I do. And I feel tired today."

Will knew quite well that Won't would dawdle along and not get back till dinner was half over, and then his mother would worry. So he jumped up himself.

"All right, I'll go," he said. "But I think you're lazy and selfish, Won't."

He went off quickly, knowing that he would not have much time to get there and back before dinner. He ran all the way and collected the clean shirts. Mrs Harris beamed. She liked Will.

"Look, Will," she said, "you go home the other way, down through the market — because there's a circus coming through the town today and that's the way they're taking. You'll see the elephants pulling the caravans, and maybe catch a glimpse of the clowns, too. And you'll hear the lions roaring in their cage."

"Oh yes — I'll go back that way!" said Will. "Thanks for telling me. How did you know?"

"I've been doing the washing for some of the circus-folk," said Mrs Harris. "That's how I know the circus is coming through the market today. Hurry now!"

Will hurried. It would be such fun to see the bright caravans belonging to the circus and to watch the big elephants pulling them along. He hoped there would be one or two clowns turning somersaults in the procession, too.

The circus was coming through the market-place just as Will got there! It was lovely. The elephants plodded slowly along, and three clowns turned somersaults and shouted merrily as the caravans passed by.

In the middle of the market-place one of the clowns climbed to the top of the drinking fountain there.

"Hey, hey, listen!" he cried. "The circus will open tomorrow night! Grandest circus in the world, four elephants, performing dogs, dancing horses, tightrope walkers, everything you want. Catch! Here are some free tickets! Use them tomorrow night! The circus is here! The circus is here!"

The people scrambled for the free tickets – and one fell right on top of Will! He grabbed at it – and there was the ticket, safe in his hand. Hurray! He could go to the circus! He rushed home to tell his mother.

But when Won't heard about it, how long his face was! "*I* haven't got a ticket," he said. "Just like Will's luck!"

His mother turned round sharply.

"Now you stop grumbling, Won't! It's nothing to do with luck! *You* would have got the ticket if you'd done as I told you and done the errand! Your laziness and selfishness stopped you seeing the procession and catching the free ticket. Will deserves it and – mark my words, Won't – unless you change your ways, this is the sort of thing that will happen to you all your life long! If you *won't* do things for others, you *won't* get the fun and excitement and treats that unselfish people get! Will will get everything and deserve it – and Won't won't!"

It served Won't right, didn't it? Will is going to the circus, and Won't will be left behind. But I really don't feel in the least sorry for him, do you?

Peter's good idea

F our children met to play each day by the village pond. They were town children, sent to stay in the country for a long holiday – and what fun they had in the fields and woods!

Peter, Jane, Tom and Bessie knew all the farm animals now. They called the horses by their names; they knew Daisy, Buttercup, Blossom and Sorrel, the prettiest cows in the field. They had been chased by Snorter the bull, so they knew him very well indeed!

They had fed the chickens and ducks; they had watched the piglets grow into fat pigs. They counted the sheep in the fields to make sure none had got out through the hedge, and they loved the tiny kids belonging to the nanny-goat on the common.

They helped to pick the plums and the apples – but now winter was coming on, and there was no more fruit to pick. The blackberries were gone. The nut trees were bare of nuts and of leaves too. There was ice on the village pond.

"I wonder if it will bear us yet," said Jane, and she tried the ice with her foot. It broke at once.

A voice shouted to them, "Now then, children, don't you be silly enough to try that ice yet! It won't be strong enough to bear you till the turn of the year!"

"I wish we had something to do," said Tom. "There's nothing to pick now. No young animals to feed. They won't let us milk the cows or clean out the sheds."

"Well, we'll be able to go sliding after Christmas perhaps," said Jane. So they waited patiently for the frost to harden the ice – but instead of the weather getting colder after Christmas, it became warmer.

"What shall we do today?" said Peter, kicking at a stone. "It's too muddy to go walking. I got my boots so covered with clay yesterday that it took me an hour to clean them this morning."

"Let's go exploring in the lofts," said Bessie. "There's nobody to say we mustn't today. The farmer has gone to market, and his wife is ill in bed."

"Well, we mustn't get into mischief," said Peter, who was the eldest. "We'll only just explore, see?"

So off they all went to explore the lofts whose dusty windows showed here and there at the top of the outbuildings.

It was exciting climbing up the rickety ladders. Some of the lofts were full of rubbish and sacks. It was fun to play hide-and-seek there. One loft was stacked with sacks of different kinds of grain. The old tabby-cat lay on an empty sack up there, purring.

"She's the guardian of the sacks!" cried Jane. "She hunts the mice that come up here. Oh, look – here's a whole nest of tabby kittens in the corner!"

That was a lovely find! The kittens all had their eyes open, and were playful. The tabby-cat let the children play with her kittens for a little while, and then she curled herself round them.

"She thinks they are tired and have had enough of us!" cried Bessie. "Well – we'll leave you alone then, Tabby! Come on – let's go and see what's in the biggest loft of all!"

Down the ladder they went, and ran to the oldest barn. They could find no ladder up to the loft there. They sniffed and sniffed, because there was a lovely smell in that loft.

"I guess the farmer has hidden the ladder," said Tom. "Maybe he doesn't want anyone to go up into this loft."

"Well, we'd better not, then," said Peter.

But the others felt as if they simply *must* explore that loft too. "We'll see if we can find a ladder," said Tom.

"I'm going off to look at the pigs," said

Peter. "I don't think we ought to go up in this loft."

He went off. The others looked after him, and half thought they would follow. But Tom couldn't bear to leave the loft unexplored. He *must* see what that lovely smell was!

The three children hunted about for a ladder. At last they found one. It was long and heavy, but they just managed to carry it between them. They got it into the barn and put it up to the loft. Then up they went, one after another.

"I say! It's the apple-loft!" cried Tom in delight. "Gosh! What a lot of apples!"

"We helped to pick them, didn't we?" said Bessie, sniffing the lovely apple-smell. "Look at those red ones – they came off the big tree by the wall."

"And those green ones came off the little trees, and the brown ones off the trees by the pig-sty," said Tom. "I say – I do feel hungry!"

So did they all, quite suddenly, as they looked at those delicious apples.

The smell got inside them and made them long to dig their teeth into the sweet, juicy apples!

"Let's take some," said Tom. "There are so many that the farmer will never know."

"But we oughtn't to," said Bessie.

"I can't help it!" said Tom. "I just feel I must!"

He picked up an apple – but it was bad on the other side, so he threw it down. He picked up another. That was half bad too.

"These bad apples are making all the others rotten too," said Bessie. "They will soon all be bad – so we'd better eat them whilst they are good!"

"We could creep up here every day and help ourselves to apples!" said Jane, who loved apples.

"Let's take one to Peter," said Tom. So he picked out a fat, red, juicy one, and put it into his pocket for Peter. Then the children climbed down the ladder and went to find him. He was by the pigs.

He liked the pigs – they were always so cheerful and friendly.

"Peter, that loft is *full* of apples!" said Tom. "We've brought one for you. Isn't it a beauty?"

"Tom! You can't do that! They are not your apples!" cried Peter.

"But, Peter, they are all going bad," said Tom crossly. "We may as well eat them whilst they are good. It's such a waste to let things go bad."

"I wonder if the farmer knows his apples are going bad," said Peter. "It's funny he lets them do that. Tom, take these apples back. Bad or good, they are not ours to take."

Tom was sulky. He didn't want to do as Peter told him. It was too bad, just when they had all thought they could munch juicy apples. But Peter glared at him so hard that Tom knew he had better obey. So he took the apples and ran back to the barn, grumbling hard to himself.

"I'll get some apples when Peter isn't

about," said Tom to himself. He threw the apples into the loft and came down again – just in time to see the farmer coming home from market!

How glad Tom was that he and the others were not eating the apples then! He went red, and wondered if the farmer would guess what he had been doing.

The farmer came over to the pigs and looked at them. Peter spoke to him. "Do pigs like rotten apples, sir?" he asked.

"Yes – they'll gobble them all up!" said the farmer. "Why, Peter?"

"Well, sir, did you know that half your apples are going bad up in the loft there?" said Peter. "They'll be turning the good ones rotten, won't they – and that's a pity."

"You're right, Peter," said the farmer. "My wife usually sees to all those jobs for me – the apples quite slipped my mind! Since she's been in bed there's been a lot of jobs left undone – and that's one. All those apples should be sorted out, and gone over every week. The rotten ones should be thrown to the pigs. Dear, dear – what a pity my wife's ill. And it doesn't help her, having to worry about all her jobs."

"*We* could do that job for you!" said Peter at once. "We could sort all the apples every week, sir. Shall we do it?"

"That would be very good of you, Peter," said the farmer. "Yes – that would certainly be a help. Get the others to give you a hand, too. Could you do it today?"

"Of course!" said Peter. He beckoned to the other three. They came up, wondering if the farmer was going to give them a scolding for going into the loft.

They were excited when Peter told them the job they were to do. It would be fun to do that, even if Peter wouldn't let them eat any of the apples! They rushed back to the barn.

"Now, Jane and I will go up the ladder and sort out the apples," said Peter.

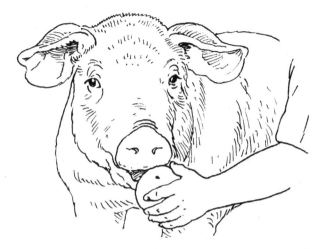

"Tom, you and Bessie must be down here and pick up all the bad ones we throw down. You can put them into the big wheelbarrow and take them to the pigs."

So Peter and Jane were soon very busy indeed sorting out the bad and good apples. Every rotten apple was thrown down to the barn below. Tom and Bessie picked them up busily, and piled them into the barrow.

It was hard work. There were hundreds of apples, all neatly set out on the floor, and every one had to be looked at. The good ones were set back, and the bad ones were thrown down.

The pigs were thrilled. Apples – and more apples – and yet more. My, what a feast for hungry pigs!

The farmer came up after a bit. "Let's see the apples you are giving to the pigs," he said. "My, they *are* bad, aren't they! That's enough for the pigs today. Keep the rest to give them each day – and come every Saturday to sort out the apples again for me. That's a good job you can do, and I shall be very grateful, and so will my wife. It will help to stop her worrying."

"We'll come along, sir," said Peter, scrambling down the ladder. "And you may be sure we shan't eat any of your apples ourselves. I'll see to that!"

"Good boy!" said the farmer. "But, my lad, you must have a little reward for your good idea! You and your friends can help yourselves to a couple of apples each, every day. There are enough apples there to feed an army, if they are well sorted out into good and bad – so you help yourselves, and choose the juiciest you can find! Children that are honest and can be trusted deserve to have a reward!"

"Oh, thank you, sir!" cried Peter in delight. "Two apples a day for each of us – that's lovely."

The kind old farmer went off to his horses. Peter looked at the others. They had gone rather red.

"Yes – I don't wonder you feel a bit ashamed!" said Peter. "You were going to take the apples without permission! And now see what's happened – we've done a good job of work, the farmer is pleased, the farmer's wife will be pleased, the pigs are pleased, and we've got permission to take more apples than we would ever have dared to eat! What do you think of that?"

"We think you had a very good idea, Peter!" said Tom. "And next time we'll have good ideas, too! Now let's eat our apples – aren't they DELICIOUS!"

Betsy-May and the giant-boy

Once a little boy called Harry came to live next door to Betsy-May. She heard him shouting to his dog on the other side of the wall, and she wondered what he was like.

"I can't see him because the wall is so high, higher than Daddy's head, even," thought Betsy-May. "But perhaps I could shout to him."

So she shouted to him: "Boy-over-the-wall! What are you like?"

There was a silence. Then Harry's voice came over the wall. "I'm a big giant-boy! Shall I look over the wall at you?"

"Don't be silly," shouted back Betsy-May. "There aren't any giant-boys."

"Well, you just see me peeping over!" said Harry. Now Harry had a pair of stilts, and he could walk on them cleverly. When he walked on them they raised him up high, and made him very tall. He ran to get his stilts, climbed up on them and walked to the wall.

And to Betsy-May's enormous surprise, there was Harry's head suddenly looking over the top of the wall at her!

"You're standing on a ladder," she said.

"No, I'm not," said Harry. "Really I'm not. Look – I'll walk down the garden, just against the wall, and you'll see my head bobbing just above the wall all the time. I tell you, I'm a giant-boy!"

Betsy-May watched. Sure enough, as Harry walked down the garden near the wall, perched on his high stilts, she saw his head bob-bobbing over it, just as if he really were a giant-boy on the other side! It was most surprising.

Betsy-May didn't like it. Harry called to her. "Well – I *am* a giant-boy, you see! Wouldn't you like to come and play with me? People don't often have the chance of playing with giant-boys."

"I don't want to play with you," said Betsy-May. "I am sure I couldn't like giant-boys. You would be taller even than my daddy and I shouldn't like it."

"Baby-girl, baby-girl!" cried Harry, looking over the top of the wall again.

Betsy-May gave a squeal and ran off. She wouldn't go near the wall again, but played with Baby James all the morning at the bottom of the garden. Mummy thought she was a very good girl indeed!

The next day Mummy said to Betsy-May: "Darling, Mrs Toms, who lives next door, has a nice boy called Harry. They want you to go there to tea today. As it is only next door, you can go by yourself. It is time you went out to tea alone now."

"I don't want to go," said Betsy-May,

making up her mind that she would never, never go to tea with any giant-boy taller than her own daddy.

"Don't be silly, Betsy-May," said Mummy, quite crossly. "You love going out to tea, and Harry is a very nice little boy."

"He isn't," said Betsy-May. "He's a horrid big boy."

"Betsy-May! Why, you haven't even seen him!" cried her mother.

"Yes, I have. When he walked down the garden, I saw his head bob-bobbing over the top of the wall," said Betsy-May. "He's a giant-boy."

"Betsy-May, now surely you aren't beginning to tell me stories," said her mother, looking very solemn. "I am sure you have never seen Harry – and as for seeing his head bob-bobbing over the wall, well, that is quite impossible."

"I don't want to go to tea with him, all the same," said Betsy-May.

"Well, I'll go with you and take Baby James, too," said Mummy. "I know

Baby James won't be frightened of a nice little boy like Harry."

Betsy-May looked at Mummy. It would be all right if she went too. So she nodded her head and said: "All right – I'll go, but you must keep hold of my hand. I don't like giant-boys at all."

Well, they went to tea that afternoon. Betsy-May couldn't help feeling rather afraid, so she held on to Mummy's hand very tightly. They went into the garden to have tea there – and, dear me, Harry seemed to be only a little boy after all, hardly any bigger than Betsy-May herself.

"You're not a giant-boy after all," said Betsy-May. "I nearly didn't come to tea with you because I don't like giant-boys."

"Shall I show you how I make myself into a giant-boy?" said Harry with a naughty giggle. "Then, if you like, you can try to make yourself into a giant-girl."

Although Betsy-May didn't at all like

giant-boys, she felt it would be most exciting to make herself into a giant-girl. So she nodded her head.

"I'd like to be a giant-girl," she said. "Baby James *would* be surprised."

Harry ran off to get his tall stilts. In a minute he came back, walking on them. They made him very tall, of course. Betsy-May stared in surprise.

"Oh! You've got stilts! You're not really a giant-boy after all! You just walked on those down the garden, and that's how I saw your head over the wall!"

"Of course, silly," said Harry. "Now you try them."

It looked very easy to walk on the stilts because Harry did it so well. But Betsy-May fell off at once. Baby James laughed and gurgled to see her. She tried again and again, and at last managed to walk a few steps. She did feel tall and grand!

Harry and Betsy-May had a fine time together, and Betsy-May was sorry when she had to go home.

"Well, will you go to tea with Harry another time all by yourself?" asked Mummy, as they went home. "Or are you still afraid of him? Such nonsense, saying he was a giant-boy!"

"One day, when you look up, you'll see a giant-*girl* peeping over the next-door wall at you," said Betsy-May. "You just wait, Mummy. You'll get a dreadful fright."

"Well, well, we'll see!" said Mummy, with a laugh. "You just try, and see what happens, Betsy-May."

So Betsy-May goes to play every day with Harry now, and is trying her very hardest to be a giant-girl on his stilts. How surprised everyone will be when she looks over the wall at them!

The boy who threw stones

There was no boy in the school who could throw better than Jock. He could throw a ball higher and farther than any other boy, and he could throw stones at anything and hit it, smack in the middle.

But he threw stones far too much. He threw them at animals and he threw them at birds. He didn't throw them at the other boys, because they punished him if he did.

"You keep your stones to yourself," said Peter, fiercely. "And let me tell you this, Jock – it's a cowardly thing to do, to throw stones at dogs and cats and birds, as you do. So just stop doing it."

But Jock couldn't stop. He always

carried a pocketful of round stones, and his hand was always in his pocket, choosing a stone to throw at the next animal or bird he saw.

When the grown-ups found out what an unpleasant habit he had, they were cross with him. So Jock gave up throwing stones when the grown-ups were about. He took walks by himself in the fields, and practised throwing stones at animals and birds there.

He threw stones at the cows and made them gallop about the field in

fright. He threw them at the sheep and they herded together in alarm. He threw them at the geese and hit one on the leg. It limped badly after that.

A small girl saw him. She called indignantly after him.

"You're a cruel boy! Stop throwing stones. One day you'll be sorry!"

"Pooh! You sound like a grown-up!" said Jock, and threw another stone, this time at a freckled thrush.

"Well, grown-ups and children think the same about a lot of things!" called the little girl. "You *will* be sorry one day!"

Jock saw a moorhen on the nearby river and sent a stone after it. He almost hit it. The little thing cried out "crek-crek!" in alarm, sank itself under the water and swam away quickly.

He threw a stone at a pretty wild duck, standing preening its feathers by the side of the water. The stone struck the duck hard on its right leg – and the duck's leg was broken!

It gave a terrified quack and flew into the air, the broken leg dangling down in a strange way.

"Oh! You wicked boy! You've broken that duck's leg!" cried the little girl, and she ran up to him and pummelled him hard, she was so upset. Jock pushed her away.

"Stop it! That was a jolly good shot of mine! Hit it bang on the leg."

"Oh, you hateful boy! That poor duck will have to put up with only one good leg for the rest of its life!" wept the little girl. "It can't go to a doctor. It doesn't know what has happened. Oh, look – it's flown down again – it's trying to stand on its poor broken leg as well as its good one. It doesn't know what has happened to it – poor, poor creature!"

"You're a silly little softy, going on about a stupid duck like that," said Jock, and he walked away whistling.

The next Saturday, he went walking by the river again, his pocket full of stones as usual. And, swimming near the water's edge, he saw a young swan – a cygnet. Out came a stone, and Jock sent it skimming so near the cygnet that it almost hit it.

But what was this? What was this enormous white creature suddenly coming up the bank towards him? Jock stood and stared.

It was the father of the cygnet, a big, powerful swan, gleaming white. It had seen Jock, and knew that he had tried to hurt the cygnet. So, fierce in defence of its young one, as all parent swans are, it had come to warn Jock off.

Jock laughed at the big waddling bird. He flipped a stone at it. And then something happened. The swan came right up to Jock, lifted one of its powerful wings and struck the boy on his right arm.

"Oh! Oh! You've hurt me!" shouted Jock, in great pain. He looked at his arm. He couldn't seem to use it. "You've broken my arm! You hateful creature! Oh, my arm, my arm!"

The swan had certainly broken Jock's arm. There was no doubt about that. The big bird went back to the river and swam away with its cygnet. Jock was left howling by the water. Then he heard a voice behind him.

It was the little girl again. "I saw all that happened. You're the boy who broke that duck's leg last week, aren't you? And today you tried to hit that cygnet. So the big swan came after you – and broke your arm!"

"Oh!" wept Jock. "What shall I do?"

"You can come home with me," said the little girl. "My father's a doctor. He can set your arm for you so that it will mend again – but nobody has set that poor duck's leg. You don't deserve help. You're a cruel boy and I don't like you – but I'll take you home to my father."

Still sobbing, Jock went with the little girl to her father's house. Soon the doctor was examining the broken arm. The little girl told him the story of how Jock came to get it.

The doctor looked stern. "Look here, my lad," he said, "if I don't mend your arm, you will never, never be able to throw stones at anything again, because your arm will be of no use to you. You have caused a great deal of harm and pain to other creatures. Can you tell me why I should mend your arm? Why should you have an arm that does so much damage? Look at my right arm and my hand. Do you know what I use them for?"

Jock didn't answer. He was feeling terribly ashamed of himself.

"I'll tell you," said the doctor. "I use this hand and arm to help those who are sick and ill, whose limbs are broken and damaged. I use it to help those who come to me in pain for help and comfort. That is what I use my arm for. You know what you use yours for. Now, just tell me – why should I mend it?"

"Oh, please do, sir," begged Jock. "I know what it feels like now to be in pain and to have a useless limb. I've had a dreadful lesson. I shan't be able to play cricket, or swim, or do anything much for a long time – but when my arm is mended, I promise you I'll never use it to harm others again. I'll only use it for good things. I promise you, sir."

The doctor set the bones of Jock's arm. Then he took him home in his car. He left him at his door, with a stern face.

"Your own doctor will see to you now," he said. "But I shall keep my eye on you, boy. My little girl was right when she said you would be sorry some day. You're sorry now – but if you're not sorry enough to keep your promise and mend your ways, you'll certainly be sorrier still in the future."

But Jock *is* keeping his promise. There are never any stones in his pockets now. He's a much nicer boy. He would really like to be friends with the doctor's little girl, but she won't be friends – yet. You see, she can't forget that duck's poor broken leg.

The boy on the bicycle

Mummy was telling the two children what to buy that morning. She was ill in bed, so she couldn't do any shopping or work.

Jane had cleaned up the little house as best she could, and Will had brought in some wood and coal for the fire. Now they were to go and do the shopping.

Jane looked down at the list of things. "I wish we could buy some eggs for you and some fruit, Mummy," she said. "The doctor said you were to have them, you know. But you haven't put them down on the list."

"There isn't money enough for them, dear," said her mother. "So I must do without. I'm lucky to have two children

175

like you that I can trust. I'd rather have that than eggs and fruit."

"I'd like you to have *both*," said Will. He fetched the basket and the two set off to the town. It was Saturday morning and very busy. Cars swept by, and errand boys on bicycles darted here and there.

Suddenly there came a cry. "Look out, there! You'll have an accident!"

The two children looked round. Down the hill came a boy on a bicycle at top speed. He seemed to have forgotten that he had any brakes to put on. He swung round the corner by Jane without putting his hand out to warn traffic. A car pulled up quickly and almost ran on to the pavement.

The boy fell off his bicycle, sat up in the road and howled. He had bruised his arm, grazed his hands and hurt his knees.

Will picked up his bicycle, which had the front wheel bent. Jane picked up the boy and dusted him down. People came round to see if he was all right, but finding that two children were seeing to him, and that he wasn't much hurt, they went away again. But the man in the car called out crossly: "Don't you come out on your bike again till you've learnt the rules of the road."

The boy was still crying. "Cheer up," said Will. "You're not hurt much. We'll take you home. Where do you live?"

"At the Big House," said the boy, pointing up the hill. "We've only just come, about two weeks ago. Oh, my poor knee!"

"It just wants bathing," said Jane. "Come along up the hill. Will can wheel your bike. Your mother can bathe your knee and bandage it."

"I want you to bathe my knee," said the boy. "My name's Mike. What's yours?"

Wiping away his tears, the boy walked up the hill with Jane and Will, telling them about his new house and the lovely garden.

"There are peaches in the greenhouse," he said. "And plums on the trees all purple and ripe. And we are going to have thousands of apples and pears."

"You're lucky," said Jane. "We have just one fruit tree in our garden, and that's an apple tree that never has any apples!"

They turned in at a big gateway and walked up the drive. It was so big that Jane felt rather scared. "I don't think we'd better come any farther," she said.

"Yes, come to my playroom," said Mike. "You said you'd bathe my knee for me. I don't want my mother to."

"Why not?" said Jane. "I always like my mother to see to me if I'm hurt."

They came to a big playroom with a garden door. They went in. There was a basin with hot and cold water at one end, and Jane went to it. She found a flannel and began to bathe Mike's knee gently.

Mike began to boast. "Did you see me

come down the hill at top speed? I'm not allowed to go out of the garden, really! Not till I'm more used to my bike. I've only had it three days. Mummy said I wasn't to go into the village yet."

Jane stopped bathing Mike's knee. She looked up at him.

"Well, your mother was quite right. See what a nasty little accident you had! You came down that hill without even putting your brakes on. You might have fallen right under that car. Your mother will be upset when she hears."

"She won't hear," said Mike. "I shan't tell her. She'll think I fell off my bike in the garden. I keep lots of things from my mother."

"Then I think you deserve to have an accident," said Will, in disgust. "Here you've got a lovely house and a gorgeous garden, and a new bike, and a sensible, kind mother – and you go off and disobey her and then say you're going to deceive her. Come on, Jane. Don't bother about his knee. He's not worth bringing home and making a fuss about!"

There was a movement at the end of the room and a man came forward. It was Mike's father. He had been there all the time!

"I was watching you two kind children," he said, "and I couldn't help hearing all you said. You are quite right to talk to Mike like that. He needs friends like you! He's a spoilt, disobedient little boy, who doesn't know how lucky he is."

"Well – he is lucky," said Jane, going red. "We've only got a little cottage – and our mother is ill, and we can't even get her the eggs and fruit the doctor says she ought to have. We're looking after her as best we can. We wouldn't dream of being silly like Mike, and upsetting her by having an accident because we were stupid and deceitful."

"You hear that, Mike?" said his father. "Now you see what sensible, good-hearted children think of you when you boast of being disobedient and deceitful. I hope you're ashamed of yourself. These are the sort of children who would make very fine friends for you – but I'm sure that now they won't want to see you again."

Mike looked as if he was going to burst into tears again. He caught hold of Jane's hand. "I was just boasting," he said. "I'd look after my mother, too, if she was ill. I'm sorry about yours. Daddy, can I get some eggs from the hen-house and some peaches and plums and take them to Jane's mother? And, please, Jane and Will, come and see me again. I haven't got any friends here."

Jane was delighted to hear about the eggs and the fruit. Just what Mummy ought to have. She smiled at Mike. "Perhaps you're not so bad as you sound," she said. "If your father likes, we *will* come and see you again, and play with you."

"And put a bit of your common sense and kindness into his head," said Mike's father. "I'd like you to do that. Come along; we'll get the eggs. And when your mother can spare you, come and play with Mike, and stay to tea."

That was how Jane and Will became friends with Mike, up at the Big House. Mike learnt a lot from them, and in return he gave them the eggs and fruit their mother needed, so that she soon got better.

Will has taught him the rules of the road and now Mike is allowed to go out on his bicycle by himself into the town. Very often he lends it to Will and Jane – and how grand they feel pedalling along to do the shopping!

They don't know it yet, but Mike's father and mother are giving them bicycles on their next birthdays. Won't it be a fine surprise!

White trousers

The teddy bear in Jack's playroom was a fine-looking fellow. He wore a red jersey, a little blue scarf and white trousers. At least, they were white when they were new, but now they were rather dirty.

He was very proud of his clothes. "You see, only the best bears have clothes," he told everyone. "Some poor bears have no clothes at all, only their fur. But I've got very nice clothes, haven't I?"

"Yes. So you must be one of the best bears!" said Angelina, the biggest doll, with a laugh. "Come here, Teddy. You've a button off your coat! The very best bears never have buttons off."

"Oh, dear!" said the bear in alarm, squinting down at his coat with his big glass eyes. "Yes, there's a button gone. Could you sew it on, please, Angelina? You really are so good with a needle."

Angelina found the button and sewed it on. The bear gave her a furry kiss. "Ooooh," she said, "your whiskers tickle me! There! You're a nice little bear, and certainly one of the best, because you're always kind and jolly!"

All the toys loved the little bear. They belonged to Jack, a noisy, untidy boy who liked his toys but didn't bother much about them. If one broke he didn't mend it but threw it away. The toys didn't like that. They thought they should be mended if they broke.

One day something happened. It was a rainy day and Jack had to be indoors. So he got out his paints and his painting book, and filled a glass with water. He stuck his paintbrush into it and then rubbed it on one of his paints. He looked round at his toys.

"I think I'll draw one of you and paint your picture," he said. "Now, who shall it be? I think I'll have *you*, Teddy – you'll be easy to draw!"

He picked up the teddy bear and put him on the table, standing up straight. The bear was very proud and pleased. Ah, now he would have his picture painted and he would be famous!

Mummy put her head round the door. "Oh, Jack – you've got your paints out. Please be careful of that tablecloth. I told you to take it off if you wanted to do anything messy."

"Oh, Mummy, I won't spill anything. I'll be careful!" said Jack, impatiently.

He drew the little bear, white trousers and all. Then he picked up his paintbrush again, rubbed it on this paint and that, and began to splash the colours on to the paper. How the bear wished he could see the picture! And then Jack moved his hand too quickly and knocked the glass of painting-water over on the tablecloth!

"Bother!" said Jack, staring at the coloured pool of water. "I must wipe it up before Mummy comes in. But what with?"

There was no cloth or duster in the room. Jack could hear his mother in the next room, and he looked wildly round for something to wipe up the mess. He suddenly grabbed the bear.

"I'll have your white trousers!" he said. And, oh dear, he tore them off the surprised little bear! He mopped up the pool of water with the thick trousers, and then covered the wet patch with his painting book. Now Mummy wouldn't know!

The bear was full of dismay. His trousers, his lovely white trousers! They had been used to mop up that water – and oh, goodness gracious, Jack had now thrown them into the fire! They burned slowly for they were damp. The bear sat down suddenly on the table, feeling quite sad.

When Jack had gone down to his tea

the bear climbed down miserably. The toys clustered round him.

"You look peculiar," said the pink rabbit. "Hadn't you better take off your coat and tie? It looks odd to wear those and no trousers."

"No, no. Let me keep my coat and tie," said the bear, holding on to them as if he thought the toys were going to take them off. "Oh, dear – my nice white trousers! Jack threw them in the fire, all wet and messy – and they've *burrrrnnnt!*"

He began to cry. The toys tried to comfort him. "It's a shame," said the pink cat. "He must feel cold without his white trousers."

"Oh, I do, I do," wept the bear. "And I'm not one of the best bears any more because I'm only half-dressed. I shall never be happy again!"

"It was mean of Jack," said Angelina, beginning to think hard. "He's a naughty boy. He does lots of things that his mother doesn't guess. For instance, she thinks he cleans his teeth night and morning and washes his neck and behind his ears with his flannel. But he doesn't."

"He *never* uses his flannel!" said the pink rabbit. "He only just splashes water on his face."

Angelina suddenly looked at the pink rabbit. "I've got an idea," she said. "Quite a good one. Why shouldn't we get Jack's white flannel and make the bear a pair of white trousers out of it? Jack never uses the flannel, so it won't matter!"

"Oh, Angelina, please, please do!" begged the bear and kissed her so that his whiskers tickled her again. "Oh, Angelina, you're the cleverest doll in the world!"

Angelina laughed. She sent the pink rabbit to climb up to Jack's basin and fetch the white flannel. It was quite dry because Jack never used it. He put it down beside Angelina. She took the pair of scissors that Jack used to cut his nails, and she began to cut the flannel!

All the toys watched her. How clever Angelina was! Snip, snip, snip, snippety, snip!

"There's one leg," said Angelina, "and there's another. And this bit is to go round his tummy, and that is for his back. My, Bear, you're going to look fine!"

It really was exciting to see Angelina make those white trousers. She sewed away with her needle, she sent Rabbit to get a button from Mummy's work-basket, and she made a nice buttonhole, so that the white trousers did up tightly.

"There!" she said. "They're finished. Try them on, Teddy dear!" So the bear tried them on, putting first one fat leg into them and then the other. He pulled them up and buttoned them. Then he walked proudly about in front of the toys.

"Perfect!" said the pink rabbit.

"They fit him beautifully!" said the toy cat. "I wouldn't mind a pair like that myself, though I suppose I'd have to have two pairs for my four legs."

"You look sweet," said Angelina, laughing. "Face-flannel trousers! Who would have thought they could look so fine? You certainly are one of the Best Bears again now!"

"What *I'm* wondering," said the pink rabbit, "what *I'm* wondering is – what will Jack say when his mother asks him how he manages to wash himself properly without his face flannel?"

"He'll have to own up for once!" said Angelina. "He'll have to say it's disappeared and he hasn't *been* washing himself!"

"Oh, I'm so happy!" sang the little bear, walking up and down. "Look at my white trousers, everyone, do look!"

So they looked – and I'd have liked to look, too. Face-flannel trousers – well, well, well!